Into the
Shadow Realms
Book 1

Hope Hill

Into the
Shadow Realms
Book 1

Hope Hill

Ink Drop Press
Chico, California

Dedicated to:

Denise Caton for making sure no one else saw this book in the state you did,

Aislinn Hanson for giving me permission to use her name,

And James "Jim Jam" Pionke, who I'm sure is watching from his corner of the cosmos.

1.
Aislinn

Aislinn geared up for an uneventful night of dreaming. She put on her purple polka dot pajamas and started her nightly ritual. Aislinn closed her eyes and focused on a glowing light in the distance. This time it was a neon green sphere.

Despite never knowing what she'd find, she always followed the rules. She opened her eyes and looked around, seeing a purple moss-covered floor. She began to explore. She wasn't allowed to talk to anyone until they spoke to her and promised to abide by the Travelers code:

1. None shall speak falsely to those who walk between the worlds, for they and they alone have the power to make or unmake.

2 Should the Traveler break an oath of which they know not, no punishments shall be dealt, for all shall journey to places unknown with rules the likes of which they've never known.

3. All younglings are granted safe passage should they agree to follow the rules of the land.

Aislinn gathered her courage and took off her socks. The moss was just as squishy as she'd imagined, but strangely warm. When she picked some up, she found it wasn't wet but it left indigo stains when squished.

Once she'd learned all she could about the strange moss-like substance, she decided to see what outfit she'd been given upon entering the Shadow Realms. Aislinn looked into a pool; her skin glowed violet and her eyes were their normal brown.

She wore a black and white striped jacket over a jade top with lime ribbons sewn on randomly, paired with a plum-colored skirt and black tights with multi-colored shooting stars trailing glitter. Again, she wondered how her outfits were chosen and why the outfit came with socks but not shoes. Thankfully, her hair was its normal black.

Done wondering about her appearance, Aislinn ventured further into the strange land. She decided to avoid the unusual denizens she believed lurked behind every plant or rock she saw. Lately, whenever she dreamed she noticed the local beings staring at her as if waiting for something to happen. Maybe it was just her appearance. She rarely looked like any of the people she saw. Yet, even the weirdest-looking creatures spoke in ways she understood.

Her current dreamscape seemed to beg her to explore. Luckily, nothing seemed to compel her to do more than satisfy her curiosity. She hated entering a world to discover its inhabitants insist she do something for them without even bothering to say hello.

Everything around her was new and exotic. No matter how many worlds she went to she never lost the sense of wonder. She never forgot the first dream where she was told she was special; because she could Travel to places in her dreams if she followed the ritual and believed. She was told belief was the most important part. Belief determined if you Traveled and enjoyed all the dream worlds had to offer or stayed behind with only a faint notion of regret and wistfulness.

Aislinn found a submerged building with no seams despite being a blend of marble and granite. An inscription was carved into the side of the building. She read it.

A day will come, bringing with it a savior of worlds, a changer of fates. They will have the power to make or unmake worlds in small and large ways. You will know them as a Traveler, one who journeys between the Shadow Realms. But choose wisely when selecting your champion, for choosing wrongly could mean the destruction of Realms. A champion will rise in the unlikeliest of places to save or destroy as they so choose.

She wondered whether this particular prophecy had been fulfilled yet or if the civilization was destroyed before this savior could be found. The prophecy warned that a champion would rise from the unlikeliest of places. *What exactly did 'the unlikeliest of places' mean anyway?* She thought as she explored the ancient building.

The stone seemed to pulse with power and the hangings were drenched in the history and importance of a bygone era. Aislinn declared herself an explorer and proceeded to search for the secret passageways she thought hid behind the lichen-covered corridors. Peering up at the walls, she noticed the lichen was red and glowing. She pulled some off and it warmed her hands and permeated the darkness. Realizing the importance of this discovery, she searched for a container. Finding a glass jar, she placed her lichen in it and picked more to fill the makeshift lamp.

She ventured into the dark corridor determined to discover what happened in these ancient walls. What made the people who once dwelled here leave? Did they choose to vanish, or did circumstances force the issue? Was it a simple desire to escape this place for a better one? Why would anyone choose to leave this fascinating dwelling if they didn't have to?

She stumbled. falling through the trapdoor she had searched for but given up on finding. She began to feel along the walls, making sure she could tell what was up ahead as she'd dropped the jar when she fell. She felt something gooey and pressed on it accidentally activating the lighting system. A series of torches filled with orange glow worms.

10

The torches illuminated the ruins which looked like an archaeologist's wish list. The room held a dazzling array of paintings, tapestries, wall hangings, statues, carvings, books, and more. The most incredible piece in the room was a globe floating above a pedestal with a sign stating the globe is a representation of Theopolis. The sign mentioned the globe was interactive and would change in response to questions but only if asked aloud.

"Theopolis?" Aislinn said as she read the inscription. "What is Theopolis?"

The globe shimmered before morphing into a line of text.

Theopolis is the name of a world long since forgotten and abandoned.

Aislinn wondered why an entire world would be abandoned. What happened to all those people? Did they leave the world behind and head somewhere else? How hard would it be to leave behind everything you've ever known to make your way to places unknown with no guarantee things would improve? Finally, another thought occurred to her. What if the globe could show what the world looked like now? Perhaps by seeing the planet she could find out if the people from there survived.

"What does Theopolis look like now?" The globe shimmered before showing her the lush landscape covered by an eerie fog the color of a blue glowstick with all the stickiness of caramel. All traces of buildings were covered with plants and all the plants were covered in that horrid fog, blanketing everything in sight. "Is Theopolis inhabitable at this moment?" The sphere again became a page with words on it.

Theopolis cannot sustain sentient life until the fog has been conquered and the air is made breathable once more.

She was horrified and determined to find out if the planet's previous inhabitants had at least escaped alive. "Did anyone escape Theopolis before it became uninhabitable?"

The globe expanded filling half the room. The globe focused on people around Theopolis meeting in large groups. Most of the groups were clustered around portals, spaceships, and anything capable of traveling off-planet. She saw them leave in droves, some crying, some laughing hysterically. No one was happy to leave but it was necessary to ensure their survival. Some remained, likely hoping they could find a way to survive or adapt to the changes their planet was enduring. Many of the people took animals and plant cuttings in case their people relocated to a planet similar to Theopolis.

Aislinn cried in relief and despair knowing, for the most part, they survived but their world may have been left behind forever. She wanted to ask more about this fascinating civilization she feared really existed.

She didn't know how her dream worlds could be real. How could she have Traveled to other Realms? What happened to her peaceful ventures into the fantasy Realms she saw in her dreams. Wouldn't she have noticed if she was entering other Realms while she slept?

Aislinn's world had been shaken and all she wanted was to go home. She was far too young to witness the death of every living thing on a planet. She knew most of the people survived long enough to escape but many would likely have died in the search for a suitable planet and with each death more of their culture was decimated. She had seen the death of a planet; a catastrophe so widespread only the plants could survive and even they had to mutate to do so.

She decided to do something she'd never done before. She ended the dream and started the ritual to return to the comfort of her home. She was going to wake up and scream so she could get her parents to hold her. She suddenly wished she hadn't told them she was old enough not to need a nightlight. Seven seemed so old when she said it but now seven seemed so young.

Aislinn closed her eyes and focused on the absence of color, operating on instinct. She'd never tried to end a dream early before. She focused once more and thought about her world. She opened her eyes to see her familiar bed and the inside of her room. Knowing she wasn't home yet since she could still feel the stone under her feet, she closed her eyes and repeated the ritual a third time. This time she also decided to dwell on how much she needed to be at home with her family. When she opened her eyes to a dark room she screamed. Her parents ran in and tried to comfort her but she was inconsolable.

They asked her what was wrong but she wouldn't tell them. She saw her brother and realized he'd hear her out before making any judgments. When he came closer, she stopped screaming and ran to him.

Aislinn looked at her brother and thought how nice it was that they shared their mother's black hair and their father's brown eyes. If her brother was meaner it might bother her to look like him, but he wasn't, so it didn't.

Alex held her while they watched their parents walk away after promising to listen if either of them decides they're ready to talk. Aislinn shuddered and made her brother promise not to laugh.

"Have you ever dreamed something so detailed you wondered if it was real?" Aislinn asked. Without giving him a chance to answer she started to talk. "I've been journeying to other worlds in my dreams for three years. Not all the worlds were nice but I always left the hostile worlds quickly. The world I went to tonight encouraged exploring. I found a prophecy about Travelers and dying Realms, but I kept looking for a trapdoor hiding a secret passageway.

"I found it by accidentally activating the lights and saw amazing artwork, but the best part was an interactive globe representing

14

Theopolis. It showed a wonderful world. I asked what Theopolis looked like now and was told it was abandoned. I asked why. The globe showed me an eerie fog that makes the planet's atmosphere unbreathable. Fearing the worst I asked what happened to its people and it showed droves of people and animals leaving the planet any way they could. Unfortunately, not everyone chose to leave and I realized I'd been witness to the catastrophe that killed every sentient being on the planet. It scared me so I came home. You believe me don't you?" Aislinn asked, wringing her hands.

"I've never dreamed like that, but I've had daydreams so detailed I forgot they weren't real." He explained. "It started as a game with an imaginary friend I named Merrick when I was five. They said they were a Traveler and could only be seen by other Travelers. Merrick said they were called the Shadow Realms and they were sent to see if they could find a Traveler as fewer and fewer were Traveling lately. They said anyone can Travel but once people stop believing they can't Travel to other Realms. It didn't take long to realize a half-completed journey was usually fatal. Afterward; they made it impossible to Travel if you had doubts." He paused.

"The need for Travelers is immense and even though people from all worlds can Travel since most Travelers only Travel for a few years they're always looking for more. Travelers are revered because they're fate-changers. Merrick said active Travelers have the power to make or unmake things."

15

"When we Travel we affect things and depending on what we do we can change things in more than one Realm. Merrick told me their real name is impossible for humans to pronounce. I think they just like being secretive but I can't prove it. Merrick told me they're from Renthyx. Merrick's a Kivexen. Travelers typically say they're a Traveler and then the planet they were born on. If the person agreed to abide by the Travelers code then they introduce themselves with their name or as close to it as they can get." Alex stopped to catch his breath.

"Merrick told me the code which I'll paraphrase for you. Those following the code agree to the following things; they can't lie outright, they can't punish you for breaking a rule you didn't know about, once you know the rules you have to follow them, children are sacred and to be protected. They phrased it weird but that's the gist of it." Alex said.

"You should let me know what you saw before entering the world and how you got there. Tomorrow I'll try to go there. If I can't then I'll do my best to find Merrick and get them to help. Can you hold out till then? Once I have some answers I'll distract the 'rents and fill you in." Alex offered.

Aislinn dried her eyes, clenched her fists, and answered with "Okay. I just needed someone to listen. I can wait but I don't think I can sleep alone after what happened. Can we have a sleepover like we used to? Please? I'm scared I'll Travel again once I fall asleep."

16

Aislinn held her breath looking up at her brother.

"If mom and dad are fine with it," Alex said with a smile.

She grabbed her blankets, a pillow, and her favorite teddy bear, then reached for her brother's hand as she used to when she was little. Alex walked them down the hall to their parents' room to let them know what was happening. He knocked and waited for them to answer. Their dad answered the door in his old robe and faded gray sweats.

"Aislinn's scared to sleep alone and asked if she could sleep in my room. Is it okay if she sleeps in my room?" He said.

Their dad turned to him and said "I'll let you two have your sleepover for now. Alex, go to your room. I need to talk to Aislinn alone for a moment. I'll walk her to your room in a minute." Alex left taking Aislinn's things with him.

Her dad looked at her and sighed. "Honey, I'm glad you trust your brother, but it's okay to ask your mom and me for help. Promise you'll come to us if you need to?"

Aislinn looked up at her dad who seemed to have aged ten years and realized he was just a man. She was so used to him being able to solve anything. Realizing that he had flaws hurt. He looked as if her saying no right now would break his heart. "I promise I'll go to you or mommy if I need to." She smiled up at him and hugged him. He grabbed her and picked her up, making sure she still had her bear. She started to drift off safe in her daddy's arms, but not before saying.

"Love you."

*****

The night was long and fraught with tension. Aislinn kept having nightmares and Alex woke their parents each time he heard her cry out. Eventually realizing they'd keep being woken up they moved everyone out to the living room. Dad made coffee and cocoa figuring it might help. They settled in for a long night, afraid to look at the clock and thankful it was Friday night and no one had anywhere to be in the morning.

Dawn came and went with whimpers, cries, tears, and the occasional scream of fear after a short nightmare. The morning dawned showing the signs of a sleepless night. Aislinn looked the worst with tear stains, puffy cheeks, red eyes, and a head full of tangles. Her brother's face was pinched though he appeared to have slept the most.

"Would you mind going to the store to get the fixings for Spaghetti, Garlic Bread, and something for the kids?" Her dad asked as her mom nodded and started writing a grocery list.

"Alexander, Aislinn I'm going to the store for a little while, be good for Daddy. Okay, where are my hugs?" Her mom asked before Alex and Aislinn hugged her.

After their mother left, the two kids looked at their dad to see what he would say to them. "I need to change, can you two play quietly for a minute." Alex and Aislinn nodded and decided to change out of their pajamas. It didn't take long so they started a quiet game of Go Fish.

"Can you keep an eye out for mom and dad while I Travel? I'm going to look for Theopolis. I'll see if I can get Merrick to help you if I don't find anything. Merrick promised to help me if I ever needed it. Watch closely to see the way I journey from Realm to Realm, maybe you'll be able to use the same method should you need to Travel during the day. If anyone asks, tell them I took a nap. I need you to do your best to wake me up before dad gets back. Repeat these words *'All Travelers must return to whence they came. Your Realm needs you once more.'* Don't paraphrase them or change the order. They have to be exact or it won't work." Alex said.

2.
Alex

Alex closed his eyes and began to chant *"I need a Realm where secrets are buried. I need to know what transpired on Theopolis. Take me to a Realm with the answers I seek. I must know what was hidden. My sister lies in the balance and I cannot leave her to face her fate alone. Please grant me the knowledge to save her."*

He pleaded. He knew the more information he gave the greater the odds of his request being granted. He saw a turquoise square. As it drew closer he realized it was a Realm though that didn't mean it was the one he needed. He saw the square become clearer and realized it was a space colony. He just hoped anyone on it would be friendly.

He entered the square through a child-sized hole and floated into a chair facing a bunch of screens showing all kinds of things. He'd heard Merrick talk about this Realm. It was home to the Observers. They were always present but almost impossible to find. They would only speak with you if you had a great need or they learned you were the subject of a prophecy.

He saw Merrick heading in his direction and almost called out to them until he realized Merrick was dressed as an Observer. Discovering one of his oldest friends had lied to him hurt. He ducked into a corridor and waited for Merrick to pass. He knew he should be catching up with them and asking questions for his sister's sake but he couldn't. Alex promised himself that if he couldn't find the information Aislinn needed, he would track Merrick down and demand answers.

He watched Merrick leave. Then he grabbed his favorite cloak; a grey, black and white one. It covered his granite patterned shirt and more importantly his blackberry-colored pants with the rust-colored details. He peered around, seeing no one he broke into the complex. Someone should have been protecting the compound but since no one appeared it must mean he was meant to be there. The thought of someone planning his or his sister's lives was frightening.

Suddenly, he saw the room he was waiting for; the command center with its interactive screens designed to see anywhere in the Shadow Realms. He asked for a viewing of what happened to his sister last night. The screen showed his sister dressed in a Traveler's outfit. All Travelers dressed oddly. Giving a distinctly alien look no matter where they venture.

She was exploring a half-buried building using orange glow worms for light while she wandered through the corridors. He saw her fall through a trapdoor and become entranced by the artifacts. When

21

she saw the globe he knew this was what caused her nightmares. He asked to zoom in and saw a plaque stating that it was an interactive replica of Theopolis. He stared even harder waiting to see what happened while keeping an ear out for the Observers.

He watched as she asked questions of the globe with its eerie semblance of sentience. He observed her finding out it was a planet. He watched her ask what happened to the planet and saw the glowing fog clinging to everything and the plants mutating and taking over everything. The blue fog was disturbing; its existence seemed unnatural.

He knew what her next question would be. The answer would be horrifying; especially since the globe would show her. He witnessed the evacuation of Theopolis and the group of people who chose to stay in the hopes of curing the fog. He watched as she found out Theopolis was incapable of supporting sentient life. He was horrified. His little sister had seen this, and even if the worst of it hadn't occurred to her, she'd still been devastated.

Seven was far too young to witness a global extinction, and Aislinn, for all her bravery, couldn't handle everything Alex had just learned about Theopolis. He wouldn't tell her that those who remained on the planet died, along with any animals left behind, or that most of the ones who left probably died before finding a suitable replacement planet.

Even if they could travel between planets it didn't mean everyone would survive the rigors of interplanetary travel. Or that all worlds capable of supporting life would have the right atmosphere for the survivors. He asked the computers to stop showing the recording. He'd discovered what he'd been looking for.

He wished he hadn't discovered what scared Aislinn. Alex became worried when he realized he didn't know how long he'd been gone. Someone was going to check on him at some point and he needed to be there when they did. The longer he 'napped' the worse it would be. He didn't want to know what a doctor might discover while he Traveled.

He quickly began to focus on what Earth looked like from space, the shape of the North American continent, an aerial view of the US, the shape of his state, his hometown, his street, his house, and finally his room. Slowly but surely he remembered every responsibility he had in his everyday life until he re-entered his room and opened his eyes. Luckily he'd entered one of the Realms where time moves slower so he'd only been gone half an hour. Right after he'd returned his dad checked on them and saw them playing Go Fish.

"Your mom's going to be back soon. Would you mind helping clean up the kitchen so we can start on dinner once the groceries are put away?" Dad asked.

"What are we having for dinner?" Aislinn asked. She wanted to know if she'd have time to talk to Alex while they cooked.

"We're having Sgetti and Garlic bread. Now it's time to clean the kitchen so mom doesn't have to when she gets home. I'll clean up the living room and I'll let you slide on your rooms till tomorrow." Dad said.

Just after they finished cleaning the kitchen their mom knocked on the door. She had so many bags in her arms she couldn't open the door. Their dad removed a couple of bags and asked them to help their mom get the groceries put away. After about twenty minutes everything was put away except what was needed for dinner.

3.
Aislinn

Aislinn grabbed Alex's arm and dragged him into her room. "I realize you won't be able to tell me everything but I'd like to know if you're any closer to having a solution. Even if you can't solve this for me I will still be grateful you bothered to try." She said hugging Alex. She smiled at him encouragingly when she saw his hesitance.

He finally answered. "I found out what upset you last night. I even found out what happened to the inhabitants of Theopolis. While I can't say what happened was pleasant. I can tell you almost everyone escaped the planet. I also know someone who can find out what happened to those who went off-world. But it may take a few days to get a hold of them."

Aislinn looked at him with a mixture of joy and relief as she laughed through the tears. "I didn't know how long it would take you to find something. Even when I try to go to a specific place, I don't always end up there. Something automatically sends me to wherever I need to go without my control. Just knowing there's someone I can talk to about everything helps. If I'd known you were a fellow Traveler I could have come to you years ago." Aislinn said, hugging her brother tight.

Dinner was announced and Aislinn ended the hug as they hurried back to the kitchen to eat. When they finished dinner they were told to rinse their dishes and put them in the dishwasher before heading to the living room. When they got there they saw their parents sitting on the couch. Mom spoke first. "Close your eyes and hold out your hands. No peeking."

Their mother placed something soft in Aislinn's hands and their father placed something hard in Alex's hands. When they opened their eyes Aislinn was holding a grey bunny and Alex had a small venom green race car. They hugged their parents and said, "Thank you!"

Aislinn grabbed her bunny and proceeded to go over as many names as she could. "Grayson, Randall, Fluffy...I know; I'll call you Vera." Aislinn said.

When Alex and Aislinn kept yawning continuously they had to go to bed. Just as their mom and dad came in to say goodnight they were told to come to get them if either of them needed anything. Aislinn was picked up and carried to her room even though they all knew she might need someone with her later on. Then with a final kiss on her head, they tucked her in and left her room keeping the door ajar so they could hear her if she got scared.

*****

When Aislinn drifted off this time she tried her brother's method of Traveling. Aislinn focused and began chanting what she wanted. *"I need a Realm that will soothe my soul. Places of refuge, a sanctuary for my troubled mind, grant me peace in the comfort of the Shadow Realms. I need a place to rest and ease my fears. I care not where I'm placed so long as there are no trials and tribulations there."* Aislinn was amazed at how easily the words came to her. Aislinn waited to see what would happen before opening her eyes as she finished the ritual by focusing on her need for comfort.

Aislinn waited for the world to appear as she whispered her plea repeatedly. She wanted to be there and help Theopolis in any way she could but she was aware of her limitations. She had cried some but how do you finish grieving something like this? How do you know when it's time to stop crying and start getting on with your life? She had never faced such grief.

Suddenly Aislinn saw a bright periwinkle sphere with large cone-shaped spikes. She came closer and saw a series of chests in every color imaginable and some she was certain she shouldn't be able to see at all. The most intriguing had no color at all just shimmers where the light hit it just enough to show the outline. She thought one might have been in the Ultraviolet spectrum. She walked towards it hoping that even if she couldn't see it she could feel it. Aislinn wondered if

27

she'd be able to see the things hidden in the trunk. She pulled out a silky cloak she couldn't see which smelled faintly of lavender. She put on the cloak only to realize she couldn't see herself.

Aislinn began to search for other treasures. She started to pull things out of the shimmery chest, closing her eyes to feel things before looking to see if they were visible or not. She gave up on searching through the box for things she couldn't see. There are only so many times you can hold something you can't look directly at. She took off the cloak and looked in a mirror at her outfit. She wore russet red pirate boots, black suede breeches, and a white long-sleeved shirt under a tan tunic with russet embroidery. Her hair was white and her skin glowed violet.

She knew the Shadow Realms didn't work like that. There weren't Realms of Piracy but some seemed to have been designed by pirates. After all, who else would be fascinated by a place where every inch of 'land' was covered in treasure chests. She laughed as she saw an entire chest of confiscated candy. She thought about the look on Alex's face if she told him about this.

Aislinn ate some of the candy leaving things she recognized alone until she'd tried other things. She was determined to enjoy the delicacies that were most alien to her. Aislinn picked up a tiny tree-like thing and not knowing if it was poisonous or not; smelled it, looked it over, and after determining that it was safe; ate it. She bit into the tree-like confectionary; it tasted like a peppery vegetable in a citrus glaze. Finding it tolerable but not desirable she chose not to eat another. She searched for a different treat and found a small metallic-smelling thing shaped like a cube. She noticed an oily residue on her fingers that appeared to come from the cube and decided to leave it alone. Thinking for a minute she decided not to eat anything else she couldn't identify.

Aislinn stopped exploring as she experienced the peculiar tugging she associated with the need to return to her corporeal form. She let the tugging pull her back and went to sleep. She woke in her bedroom grateful for the respite from night terrors. She was glad she'd been allowed to sleep in later than normal. She looked at the clock shocked to realize it was almost one o'clock and quickly got dressed in a green striped shirt with flower patches and a pair of jeans.

She quickly put her jammies in the hamper and started to search for her family. Alex was in his room playing with his new race car. "Where are mom and dad? I wanted to ask them something." Aislinn asked him.

"Talking to each other. Lunch is in the microwave. I got in contact with my friend. They'll help you for as long as you need. Merrick needs a couple of days to sort things out so you'll have to act normal till they get here. Merrick will try not to appear unless it's in the Shadow Realms or we're alone." Alex said.

Aislinn's jaw dropped. She'd known he'd work hard to help her any way he could but he'd done it quicker than she thought possible.

"Thanks. I know I haven't told you everything yet but I haven't tried to hide anything from you besides my ability to Travel. But since you didn't tell me either, I doubt you care." Aislinn said.

Alex chuckled. "I didn't want to upset you if it turned out you didn't have the ability as well. I was told as I got older my ability to spot another Traveler would get better. If you don't know what you're looking for it can be hard to know when you've found it. Merrick told me our parents probably Traveled as children. I still don't know why some people Travel and others don't. Let alone why some people stop Traveling after only a few journeys yet others Travel until mid-adolescence or in rare cases adulthood." Alex admitted.

Aislinn giggled, picturing an adult trying to enter the Shadow Realms through imagination. Most adults wouldn't know creativity if it danced towards them wearing a tutu while reciting limericks. She smirked at the thought before remembering her dad made a living off his creativity.

"If I'd turned out not to have the ability knowing you had adventures I couldn't join you on would have upset me. I'd have gotten over it as long as you promised you'd always come home. I don't know what I'd do without you. I know I don't need you to protect me from everything but I don't want you to disappear. I'll always need you even if it is just to talk to." Aislinn admitted.

Alex sighed before responding. "I'm glad we can share our adventures or at least the stories of them. So much has happened and at some point, I'll tell you all of it. I'll always be available to help you. After all, I only have one sister and she's not replaceable." He said with a gentle smile and a serious tone.

Aislinn smiled happy that she and Alex were on the same page. She was excited to find out what places he'd visited and discover what advice he could give about Traveling. Thinking quickly as she heard the footsteps down the hall get louder she spoke softer. "Mom's coming. I'll tell you what happened over a round of Go Fish." Alex handed her nine cards, took nine cards, and placed the rest of the deck on the side.

She placed down a pair of threes and grabbed two cards before asking for an eight. He said Go Fish and she picked up a seven. He put down a pair of nines and grabbed two more cards, he then asked for a two which she handed over, he asked for a ten and she said Go Fish. He picked up a two and put the cards down. He grabbed more cards till he had a full hand again and their mom came down the hallway heels clicking on the hardwood floor. Just as they returned to their game and started bantering their mom came and checked on them.

"Can we join in for a game or two?" Their parents asked. Alex and Aislinn pretended to deliberate before nodding and handing them the cards to shuffle. They pulled out a second deck and shuffled it.

*****

She wanted to dream her way into a world of adventure, something she'd been terrified of the night before. She wondered if she could convince Alex to meet up with her during some of their Travels. He wouldn't want to spend every journey with her; some of the places he'd go wouldn't be nearly as much fun for her but she still wanted to go with him. Then they wouldn't have to worry about who heard them.

She closed her eyes and thought furiously about other Realms. Thinking about going somewhere she'd never been. She almost didn't notice the eye-searing tangerine trapezoid. The novelty made Traveling exciting. She loved seeing new landscapes like the orange ocean and teal trees surrounding the taupe landscape.

If it wasn't safe she wouldn't have been allowed to enter. She saw what looked like vending machines with odd instructions. She placed soil in a vending machine and was rewarded with a teal trapezoid fruit. It tasted incredible. She laughed as she remembered that she broke the laws of physics every time she Traveled within the vastness of the Multiverse known as the Shadow Realms. She'd always known that she belonged to more than just Earth; perhaps it was time she started to prove it.

She knew she'd need to solve things at some point. She wasn't helpless and she was bound and determined to prove it to the Shadow Realms. They wanted a savior and she knew it wasn't her. But why did she have to save the Shadow Realms to prove her worth? Far more important to prove it to herself than the nameless, faceless, masses. Their hero would appear and it didn't have to be her. She'd already changed things in small ways merely by being alive. She couldn't help but be herself and other Travelers had thanked her before for accelerating change. Granted the things she'd done could have happened sooner or later but she made them happen faster.

Alex may have unintentionally altered her methods of Travel permanently. She felt down to her soul that her fate and her brother's were inextricably linked. His choices would always affect her and her choices would always affect him even when they were in different Realms. She wanted to explore everything, one Realm at a time.

Aislinn loved the idea of going to places no one else could. She didn't want to map things out but she'd like to write a guidebook for the Shadow Realms. It could tell everyone which planes to avoid and which ones would be easiest to enter for each species since not all Travelers are human. These were her people, the ones for whom creativity was written all over their psyche. She needed to know why this was calling her. Why she suddenly needed to explain something ethereal.

She'd never felt such a strong urge before and was hesitant to follow it. No matter how cool it sounded if it wasn't her idea she didn't want to do it. So putting aside the decision she decided to explore. She looked at the teal trees and saw a grey fruit she was slightly afraid to eat. She could have sworn the thing had teeth and was looking at her. Yet every time she looked it appeared to be an ordinary fruit. Well, as ordinary as an alien fruit could get.

She saw a ripple in the ocean as a red creature peered up checking to see if anyone was watching. The creature looked at her for a few seconds before going back into the ocean.

She wondered if she should follow it. The red being was either shy or antisocial. She didn't want to get in the way of an unofficial science experiment again.

Last time things hadn't ended well. She didn't need to be captured again. She'd nearly forgotten that encounter, after all, she'd only been four Terran years old. This Realm was interesting but she wasn't sure she'd have come here if she'd had a choice. She'd needed some rest after the weekend she'd had. Luckily school would start soon and bring distractions from what happened to Theopolis. If she didn't know the planet was uninhabitable she'd want to visit Theopolis. From the moment she'd seen Theopolis she'd wanted to be there. She'd known that her future was there.

She'd rather be on Theopolis than anywhere. Even if she wasn't the champion the planet so desperately needed perhaps she could help in some small way. Maybe she'd even meet this '**saver of worlds and changer of fates**' and point them in the direction of places that needed their help. The more she thought about it the more she realized anyone could be their champion.

After all, everyone who Travels has the power to 'save worlds and change fates' even if most only did so in small ways. The non-champions who changed fate and saved worlds did so in ways that would have happened anyway. They accelerated inevitable things.

She decided to ask every Traveler she met if they knew how to save Theopolis. Sure the odds were against her meeting someone with an idea of how to fix Theopolis but it couldn't hurt to try could it?

She remembered her brother saying he knew a Traveler who might be able to help. Perhaps she could ask them what to do about the state of Theopolis and if the situation was likely to get worse any time soon. She had to do something after all, if she didn't, who would? Other than her and Alex she doubted anyone knew Theopolis had been destroyed.

She spent some time trying to remember when if ever she'd wanted to write a book. Unable to come up with an answer she wondered if she'd ever thought of writing a guidebook. She realized that even though she hadn't thought about writing a book she'd been telling stories for years. Wouldn't it be funny if some of the 'fiction' books she'd read before were actually nonfiction but so unbelievable they were marketed as fiction? She knew if she was to write and publish a book about the Shadow Realms it would be labeled fiction. After all, who would believe you could Travel to other Realms?

She continued to explore. She'd never seen anything like it. The non-spheroid planets were few. She'd never seen one before, though she did remember Alex telling her about the Observers and their cube colony used to record everything. Come to think of it she wondered if they were the same Observers involved in the incident years ago. She'd never seen their Realm but she probably wouldn't have been intrigued by staring at screens. She was determined to enjoy herself on this trip and she'd already wasted time wondering about past events.

Besides, she didn't know how fast time went here. She'd wasted precious time pondering things. If she wasn't careful her mental age would get too far ahead of her physical age. The effects so far were minimal; merely an advanced vocabulary and a tendency toward 'old soul' behavior. Right now she was simply deemed precocious but if it accelerated enough it could be disastrous. Realms forbid they try to make her socialize with those her age. Most of them seemed far too young.

Once more she walked along the shoreline and deciding to take a risk dipped her fingers into the orange ocean. It didn't feel like water; it was more like a gelatinous force than an ocean. She knew this Realm would be different but this was turning out to be one of the strangest Realms she'd ever been to. She thought maybe the ocean was sticky since there was nothing to cause real changes in the tide and its orbit was too slow to affect the ocean in any noticeable way.

She climbed a pale teal tree and deciding to avoid the potentially lethal fruit examined the leaves which were an intriguing blend of blues and greens in a mottled pattern. She was amused at the thought that even trees in this Realm were designed for protection from predators. She'd be willing to bet no one had been here in quite some time since the creature didn't recognize her as a Traveler. She wished it had stayed so she could try to talk to it.

She knew wishes were dangerous and tried not to mention them anywhere in her dreams. They never turn out the way you want and often cause more harm than good. She'd much rather be an architect than an archetype. She didn't need to be a princess; it seemed like they spent all their time waiting for someone to save them. She didn't want that even if it would be fun to play in the towers, turrets, and trap doors leading to the inevitable secret passageways. She knew she shouldn't rag on them, sometimes they did cool things, but mostly they annoyed her.

She wanted to see someone or something, anything to break up this terrifying monotony and frightening silence. She found the lack of noise vaguely menacing. As if someone or something was out there waiting for her to let her guard down. She wanted to run away. Something was very wrong here. The red creature was the first clue that she should have run away. Well if she ever did manage to write a guidebook she'd have to make sure she mentioned the oddities of this Realm and the menacing feel. She didn't want anyone else to run afoul of this Realm. It might not be outwardly aggressive but something here meant her great harm. She'd never encountered something so eager to inflict violence.

It might be best if her brother were here or if the Observers were to realize something was wrong and decide to investigate. She wanted desperately to escape but somehow she knew she couldn't until it was finished. The feeling of wrongness grew with every passing moment. She didn't think she could die here but she had no desire to test it.

She screamed mentally, tears rolling down her face as she faced the overwhelming fear and despair. She didn't care where it came from as long as it left soon. She could only wait for enough time to pass before someone would come to wake her from one of the scariest dreams she'd ever had. She had to do something but she couldn't force herself to do anything about it. What if she didn't wake from whatever kept her frozen?

She felt fingers clutching her shoulders trying to rouse her. Her dad pleaded. "Please, come back to us. We need you. You're scaring me. Please, come back." He finally quit pleading and just stroked her hair.

4.
Alex

Alex watched his sister's body wracked with fear and begging for help. He didn't know how to wake her without causing their parents to get suspicious. If only he could remember if Merrick told him how to bring someone back to their home Realm.

He hadn't listened when he should've and now Aislinn was paying the price. He wanted to call Merrick but wasn't sure he could count on them to fix things. He walked to his room while his parents were distracted. He shoved his anger down and focused on the fact that a youngling's life hung in the balance. He hoped it would be enough.

He had no time to second guess himself. He closed his eyes, meditated in his room, and called. "I summon thee Merrick protector of younglings and Travelers. One charged with helping whenever asked by one with just cause. I charge thee with finding the lost youngling. They need thy help. I fear their life will end if they remain lost. The Traveler was expected back hours ago and is trapped by something I can't fight or find." Alex implored.

Merrick appeared as Alex was deep in contemplation. He was shocked by Merrick's appearance but realized Merrick had been disguised when he first met them. Alex wasn't sure if Merrick would ever admit which of their many forms showed their actual appearance. This time their skin was grey with rose symbols covering most of their body, and their eyes were orange. They had four limbs with longer arms than legs and walked upside down with their head facing the ground, but they flipped themself back around to sit down. Their skin had a polished stone-like texture as did their jasper-like hair. They looked like they were made of stone and their voice was more guttural than Alex remembered. He was afraid to find out what had caused such a drastic change in appearance.

"What's wrong? I thought I taught you all you needed to know to Travel. Your message pulled me out of the Realm I was in." Merrick said.

Alex sighed and quickly told them what they needed to know. He'd save the rest for later. "Aislinn's Traveled and hasn't returned. They've been gone for hours and won't wake up. I was planning on asking for you to help with something Aislinn witnessed but now it looks like my sibling's trapped somewhere. Can you bring Aislinn home?" Alex begged.

5.
Merrick

Merrick was concerned they wouldn't be able to locate the child. Merrick tried not to imagine the devastated look on Alex's face if they failed to save Aislinn.

Merrick came out of their musings to the rough shaking of a desperate youngling.

"How do you know they're afraid? Were you with Aislinn when they got trapped? Can you tell me anything about where they are?" Merrick asked hoping they'd at least have a starting point so they could get there before time ran out.

Alex sighed in frustration. "I wasn't with Aislinn when she Traveled tonight. I've never Traveled in my sleep and don't know how she does it. She taught herself everything she knows about Traveling. Her methods are so intuitive I'm not even sure she could explain them. If she could leave, she would. No one stays near something this terrifying. I can't tell you where her spirit is but I can take you to her body. There should be a link between it and wherever

41

she is. Be careful." Alex insisted.

Merrick smiled, reaching out to hug Alex, and ruffle the kid's hair. "When things calm down we're going to have to talk about pronouns. I know what you meant and don't care much but other shapeshifters might take offense." Merrick chided.

Alex nodded. "Sorry."

"Seeing Aislinn's body would help, and as long as I don't want non-Travelers to sense me, they won't. I'll do my best to bring Aislinn home."

Alex guided Merrick to Aislinn's body. Merrick used the link to follow Aislinn into the Shadow Realms.

Merrick walked towards Aislinn. "Help! There's something wrong with this place. It's too quiet and it feels wrong but I can't leave." Aislinn admitted.

Merrick was stunned the child created a mind-link despite being self-taught. They were going to petition for the right to make Aislinn and Alex their apprentices. Yeah, they'd 'trained' Alex but they'd been told to limit what they taught. After months of nagging, they were allowed to stay with Alex and agreed to revisit the idea of taking Alex as an apprentice later. Still, they should probably answer Aislinn while the link was still open.

"My name is Merrick. Alex sent me." Merrick asked.

"Hang in there, I'm going to do my best to get you out. I need you to stay as calm as possible." Merrick said in the gentlest voice they could muster. They saw some of the fear leave Aislinn's eyes before returning. They could feel something seeking to manipulate them into leaving.

Merrick was nearly always confused by this family. They'd initially started with Kane, not that anyone knew that since Kane was only eleven at the time. The family had been Traveling for generations and were prone to Traveling long after their peers stopped. Aislinn was gifted but they wanted to train Alex more. Most thought it was foolish as Aislinn had so much potential but they'd been friends with Alex first. Besides, neither sibling would agree unless the offer applied to both of them.

Alex taught them the value of love and affection; what it meant to swear an oath and keep it. Aislinn would likely teach them as well. Merrick looked around and remembered that they shouldn't take their eyes off their surroundings.

They turned to Aislinn and waited for the child to return from the depths of their mind. "I need you to listen to me very carefully. I'm going to summon the things I need to get you home. Don't worry if it takes me a few minutes to respond. I just need to make sure I have everything with me before I do anything." Merrick assured her.

Merrick looked around, turning when necessary wondering where they put things. They knew they'd left their satchel in the Zipper Space but where had they stashed the Zipper Space. It was supposed to be bonded to them but it had a habit of hiding. Sometimes they wondered if the pocket dimension they called Zipper Space might be sentient and messing with them. It would explain why it took so long to find things they'd stashed in Zipper Space.

Finally, they located the annoying pocket dimension and began trying to retrieve things. They reached up and grabbed a speck of light only they could see, pulled it closer, and proceeded to pull the edges apart as if trying to unwrap it. When it was large enough they poked through it in hopes of finding their monster hunting supplies. They felt around and brushed up against something furry, putting it away they resumed their search before thinking 'Wait a minute. What's my cat doing here? Oh well, I'll deal with that once we're off this forsaken place.'

Finally locating the satchel they pulled it out and began to fold the pocket dimension back up before thanking Zipper Space for protecting their things. Merrick turned back to Aislinn holding their satchel. Merrick reached into the satchel and pulled out pieces of Silver which they placed in a circle around them and Aislinn. They then grabbed pieces of Iron and made a ring of it around them. When that was done they did the same thing in the third ring of Rock Salt making sure none of the rings touched.

Most of this would fail but telling Aislinn that wouldn't help. They'd deliberately chosen items Aislinn would recognize as useful against monsters. As long as Aislinn thought the objects had power they would. They only needed to escape the lurking menace not defeat it. The important thing right now was to make sure everyone survived the encounter.

Now all they had to do was convince the kid to escape. The easiest way to do so would be to mention how worried Alex is. The things Aislinn would do to spare Alex pain were the stuff of legends. Their loyalty would be one the bards would sing of for eons.

"Focus on everything waiting for you at home. Remember what it felt like to follow the link between your essence and your body. Alex is worried sick about you and I'm sure your parents are too. Try to remember how you return to Earth and the people who love you." Merrick said trying to convince the child to return. Merrick wanted to leave and inform the Observers so this planet and whatever had trapped the youngling could be dealt with.

6.
Aislinn

She opened her eyes to see her happy-go-lucky dad bawling. She might have teased him on any other day but at this moment all she wanted was for him to tell her everything would be alright. She knew it wasn't true but she still needed to hear it. "I had a nightmare." She said. Her family held her tight as they all whispered reassurances.

Perhaps Merrick would teach her what she needed to know. She was a child and she'd started to come to a disturbing conclusion about her Travels. She was beginning to think more was going on than just exceedingly vivid dreams. Perhaps what was happening in her dreams was real.

The thought nearly made her puke as she realized that meant all the bad things she'd witnessed recently would also be real. She didn't know if she wanted to Travel if it meant she'd have to encounter horrors as well as miracles. If the magical lands were tempered by horrific beasts would it still be worth it? She'd always thought herself safe being a Traveler and youngling with the added protection of having invented the places.

If they were real that would explain why everything that happened recently affected her so much. She hoped she was wrong but she'd have to ask Merrick first. As an experienced Traveler, they would know which things were real and which were not.

She searched the room looking for them and saw nothing but then again who said she'd be able to find them if they didn't want her to. She hoped when she got a spare moment she could ask Alex how to locate them. She needed to ask them these questions. Even if they didn't mean to answer her questions their body language might give them away. If she could even read their body language. If all of this was real would that mean Earth was fake? Or would it merely mean Earth was one of many planets and this universe was part of a larger multiverse?

She wished her parents could help her with this but she didn't want to scare them. The odds of keeping such a large secret from her parents were slim to nil but she had to until revealing her secrets wouldn't devastate everyone.

She waited for them to let go so she could speak without her voice being completely muffled and decided to ignore her pride and ask for the one thing she thought would help. "I'm too scared to sleep right now but maybe if I have a nightlight I'll be able to drift off. Please, Mom? I know I'm supposed to be brave. I promise it's only for tonight." She pleaded.

"I think I might know something that would work better. You remember those CDs your unt Talia made for you and the blankets sent by Aunt Paisley?" Her mother asked.

Aislinn looked at her family confused. She saw their encouraging looks and the grin that spilled across her father's face. She figured it couldn't be too bad if it made her dad smile. "Yes, mom. I remember getting CDs from Auntie Talia and blankets from Auntie Paisley but I don't remember what we did with them." Aislinn admitted.

Her mom smiled before answering. "You'll see and I guarantee you'll like it. I put them up wanting to wait until you were older to have them. Talia created some of the most beautiful lullabies I've ever heard." Her mom said with a smile.

"Follow me." Their mother told them as she headed towards the attic. "We're looking for a box labeled 'Handmade Memory Blankets' and another labeled 'Sentimental'." Their mom said. "I used to play these CDs whenever you were having trouble sleeping. I think it's why you like classical music." Their mother teased. "Talia used to play Second Violin in the C.H.O.I.R.. They used to be a big deal but I could never remember what they stood for. They still keep in touch with her and now and then they beg her to play with them." Their mother added.

"I still remember the last C.H.O.I.R. concert she performed in. You both had strep. Your dad said the concert would probably help you sleep. We bundled you up and headed out."

Their father poked his head up from one of the boxes and asked their mom a question. "Are you going to help me look or not?" He asked.

Aislinn and Alex looked at their parents and they all started laughing before continuing the search. They found the CDs in a box labeled 'Broken Ornaments'. Their dad smirked before turning to look at his wife and commenting with a trace of sarcasm. "Honey, how could you? The kids could have looked through this? How did you know they'd leave such an amazing box alone?"

They looked for blankets in the strangest places; a giant box labeled 'Dream catchers' held sports memorabilia, clothes with school logos on them, tiny pairs of socks in various colors, handwritten notes, and other random treasures. Finally, their mother found the handmade blankets with their interesting patterns and eye-catching embroidery. Their dad told them to come into the living room and get the blankets set up while he made Hot Chocolate. Their mom took some normal blankets and placed them with an abundance of pillows into a nest formation. She gestured for Alex and Aislinn to prop themselves against the sides of the nest.

Their mom covered Alex in a dark blanket with alternating colors of black, blue, and purple. The embroidery was white thread mapping out the constellations and each planet or sun was embroidered in the appropriate color. Paisley even managed to find special thread colors for asteroids and the rings of Saturn were colored separately. Aislinn's blanket had mountains and castles in the background. The real beauty though was the embroidered dragon guarding the castle and the knight in full armor with long black hair. They were so fascinated by the blankets they didn't notice their father until he handed them their drinks and sat down next to them.

"Before you were born, a group of siblings was having trouble sleeping. The youngest kept having horrible nightmares. The whole family would try to calm him. He'd wake the house two or three times a night. Finally, after weeks of nightmares, the parents asked what they could do to help him sleep. He said the dreams disappeared when he was held but when he was alone he got scared again." Their dad paused.

"So they hatched a plan. The next night they asked their children to get ready for bed and then come to the living room. They found pillows and blankets arranged like a nest. They placed the girls together and the boys together before covering them in the rest of the blankets and handing over stuffed animals. If this goes on too long we'll have to consider other options." Their dad said with a smile.

"Dad, this is a nest, isn't it? You knew the boy with nightmares didn't you?" Alex asked. Their dad grabbed the mugs and put them in the sink. While the dishes were soaking their dad tucked them in.

"Yes, Alex I did know the boy who kept having nightmares. The boy was your uncle Levi. He couldn't sleep and your grandparents created a 'nest' for him. They thought if he could get a few nights without nightmares he wouldn't be afraid to go to sleep. Talia started playing lullabies because of Levi's nightmares and Paisley came up with the idea of special blankets that defeat bad dreams. Her first blanket was a disaster; we put it in the playroom as a rug. The first successful one had a black background with bright stuffed animals made of fabric scraps. Levi still has it. He told her it was a collectible and he'd keep it for his children but we know why he kept it." Their dad said with a smile.

Alex looked at him before asking the question they all needed the answer to. "Did Levi ever figure out how to stop his nightmares?"

Their dad looked at him and answered quickly. "Yes, Levi did stop having nightmares eventually. As far as I know, he never told anyone what they were about. I know Aislinn will get through this. But it would be easier to solve the problem if we knew what was causing the nightmares. On an unrelated note, do you want to visit your relatives this week? We thought the visit might lift your spirits." He said.

7.
Alex

When his dad looked like he'd leave without finishing the story he grabbed his pant leg and shook his head, hoping his dad would realize he wasn't ready to be alone yet. His dad seemed to understand because he sat down again.

"Levi slept in the nest with all of us for three nights. After a week I could make a small nest in our room and crawl out after he fell asleep without him having nightmares. A week later he slept the whole night in the nest without me. A week later he could sleep in his bed most nights." His dad paused.

"We might not have been having the same nightmares as Levi but seeing him so scared made it hard for us to sleep. It's why I'm worried about you." His dad admitted.

Alex never knew how rare it was for a father to talk to his son like that. His parents encouraged independence in their children. Alex was used to being talked to as if he was intelligent but never before had his father talked to him man to man.

His last thought before falling asleep was that no harm would befall him in the nest as his parents would spend the night protecting them. When he woke he saw his sister clinging to him as if he represented the safety she'd been searching for. He wondered what would happen when the nest was taken away.

Alex was pulled from his musings by his sister's mumbled 'What time is it?'. He tucked her in and whispered soothing words. The outside world could wait a few hours. He let her burrow into his chest and held her close.

When he was scared as a little child and worried things would continue to get worse his father told him something he never forgot. 'Happy endings take hard work. If you don't like how your story's turning out work to make a happy ending.' Those words brought him comfort when he looked at his sister and remembered what she'd gone through. He didn't know how to fix things but he did know he could make his own ending.

He only hoped someone would be able to help them. He needed to be trained as much as she did. She needed guidance after everything that happened. If no one appeared in the next few days he'd make someone help. He didn't care if the Observers sicced the council on him. His fate was tied to hers. His last view before slipping into slumber was of his family holding each other close.

*****

He woke up once more only to feel his sister slip out of the nest and when she didn't slip back in he opened his eyes. He looked for his parents and saw them curled up together and went to make himself cereal. He grabbed his favorite cereal and poured in some milk. He left the box on the counter and sat down to enjoy his meal. Aislinn came in completely dressed and he made her a bowl of cereal so she wouldn't make a mess.

They ate their food in silence before putting the dishes in the sink where Alex washed them before putting them in the strainer. Seeing that his parents were still asleep he went to his room to get dressed and came out in a tee-shirt with a bunch of people in lab coats on the front, the back said 'these were some of the best scientists, They didn't have a picture of me when they made this shirt' and cargo shorts with black sneakers and blue laces. While it wasn't as striking as his sister's outfit he preferred a more 'toned down' look. She'd donned an orange plaid dress with a ghost-themed belt. She had orange leggings with yellow sandals.

When he left his room he found Aislinn waiting for him. "If you want to know what happened you should ask now. I don't think mom and dad will leave us alone again any time soon." Aislinn said.

"Will you tell me what you went through? I can't help you if I don't know what happened." He pleaded.

She told him slowly. "I landed on a trapezoid planet made of browns, teal, tangerine, and silvers. It took me a while to realize I shouldn't be there. I saw a red creature that seemed shy and disappeared. I kept getting distracted…the next thing I remember is feeling terrified. I tried to leave but I couldn't. I was paralyzed with fear. I couldn't return to my body. Whatever was wrong didn't want me going anywhere. I'd never felt so scared." She explained.

"You shouldn't have been able to go to a place with something capable of keeping you from leaving. Even the Council is aware of the dangers of preventing a Traveler from returning to their body. They passed a rule about it centuries ago." He insisted.

"How can you be so calm about this? I mean you're about to have your entire life changed, our parents will hover over you for months and you've witnessed homicidium planetae. Surely you don't think you'll be able to pretend to be unaffected. Even if the 'rents believed you I wouldn't. I know what happened to you and I'm not going to act like it was unimportant. What you witnessed traumatized you." Alex said in the most serious tone he could muster.

Aislinn looked sadly at her brother. "I'm not calm. Inside I'm breaking but it won't do anyone any good if I admit it. None of this is resolved and I promised myself I'd do my best to see it through. The world is a dangerous place and the Shadow Realms are no exception. I know it traumatized me but I need to find a way to deal with it." She said softly as if each word sapped her of strength.

Alex looked at her wanting to respond but unable to find the words to explain how he felt. He reached out to hold her. He spoke up before he lost his nerve. "Would you like me to do your hair today? It would allow you to be ready before the 'rents wake up. I could do whatever you want with your hair and we could use any of the accessories you'd like." He suggested.

Aislinn grabbed his hand and dragged him into the bathroom where she pointed to the cabinet she couldn't reach. "My hair accessories are in the purple box with flower stickers. Will you put my hair into pigtails with the daisy hair ties and my silver stripey headband?" She asked.

He looked around and grabbed the box, selected the daisy hair ties, and her headband. He pulled out her hairbrush. When that was done he sat down motioning for her to sit in front of him. From there he proceeded to brush her hair before separating it into two sections. He placed the first in front of her left shoulder and kept the second half behind her right shoulder. He then separated the right half into three sections which he began to braid together. Soon he was done with the first braid and tying it off. He repeated the process with the left half before tying it off. Finally, he placed her headband in front of her ears where it could contrast with the daisy hair ties. He patted her on the head before standing and pulling her up with him as they left to see if their parents were awake.

56

8.
Aislinn

What would her parents think if they could hear her now? If they knew everything she'd been through? Who cries for your misfortunes when no one knows what you've been going through? Who dries the tears they've never seen? How do you grieve for something you can't explain? She wondered as her thoughts whirled in a spiral of confusion, helplessness, and self-doubt. She tried to think about what she should say but the thoughts became too much.

Trying to avoid the truth she tried to change the subject. "Do you think the cousins will be happy to see us?" She asked.

"Honey, your cousins will always be happy to see you but your mom and I would like to let you know you can ask us anything. We promise to respect your questions and answer to the best of our abilities." Her dad said.

Aislinn looked down at her feet feeling embarrassed by her behavior. She wished she hadn't let them see her vulnerability. She'd wanted to show her family she wasn't fragile. She'd asked her family to help her with her night terrors but couldn't admit why she had them. How could she tell her family that she Traveled to other worlds in her dreams and the things she'd seen terrified her?

When they returned from their musings they began to discuss the upcoming trip. "Would you guys like to know when we're leaving to head towards Grandma and Grandpa Smith's house?" They asked.

Alex looked at her as if asking for permission to speak for her. She nodded in assent and he spoke. "Whatever's easier." He said with a shrug.

"Pack as if we'll leave at a moment's notice." Her dad said.

"What should we pack?" Aislinn asked.

Her mom smiled. "At least a week's worth of clothes."

She and Alex rushed to their rooms and began to place things in their suitcases. They placed their clothes at the bottom of the suitcases, a few books on top, and added one toy each leaving plenty of room for other things. The backpacks held journals, and things to occupy them on a long trip. When Aislinn thought she was done she asked her mom to check her suitcase.

Since her parents were in their room packing up Aislinn began the long-awaited discussion. "I don't know whether or not we should admit everything to the Cousins or just tell them enough to get the help we need. We still have Merrick to ask as a backup plan.." She said.

"Don't worry about talking to the cousins. All we have to do is tell them the truth. If they need more information we'll provide it. Dad says happy endings take hard work and it's up to the characters in the story to determine whether or not to help the story end the way it wants to. Our story isn't over; it's just begun. So dry your eyes and prepare to enjoy your vacation. If you want to get the 'rents off your back you need to show 'em you're not fragile." Alex insisted.

This conversation changed her life. It made her determined to follow him on his adventures and allowed her to face the nightmarish dreams. She lacked the words to explain this to her brother so she hugged him.

"I need to let my friends know I'm going to be out of town for a while. You'll get through this. When all else fails you'll always have me." Alex said, giving her one last smile before leaving.

She wanted to tell him how she felt about him putting off hanging out with his friends to comfort her. But the words never came out right. She walked to her parents as they granted Alex permission to hang with his friends for an hour or two. She watched him head out secretly wishing she had friends. She had the Cousins but it wasn't the same. Sometimes she wondered if the Cousins would spend time with her if she wasn't family.

She knocked on her parents' door wanting advice. When she saw them open the door she nearly lost her nerve. Steeling herself she spoke softly still unsure how to explain. "I was wondering if there's something I can do for Alex? He's been so helpful and he's even sacrificed time with his friends to help me." She watched her dad look puzzled.

"You could write him a card and try to help when you see him having trouble. However, he may feel it's his responsibility to help you." He said with a soft smile creeping up his face.

She smiled as her father pulled her into a quick hug. She reached her room and pondered the questions she'd ask the Cousins and Merrick. She suspected she'd be seeing more of Merrick in the coming months.

*****

Soon it was time for bed. She slept deeply and didn't wake despite being moved to the car. She woke to the smell of fast food. She had no idea where they were but smiled when she saw she was at a truck stop because it meant they'd be seeing the Cousins soon.

She scarfed down her breakfast sandwich and downed her OJ before looking out the window. She saw Alex stretching his legs and joined him. She headed back to the car when her mother called for them. They got back in the car and listened to the radio before she fell asleep again.

When she woke the summer sun and the beauty of the clouds sprawled across the sky. She saw the clouds morph into things. The more she concentrated the clearer the images became. She took the pictures and made stories. She never told anyone what stories she created.

She tried to focus on the lunch she'd been given. She ate the burger quickly and wondered why no one noticed she'd been so silent. Perhaps they'd gotten used to her brooding. Was it normal to feel so empty?

She tried to discard the melancholy mood that had overtaken her. But the more she struggled the worse it got. She tried to drown out her thoughts with a good book. Unfortunately, it was one of the ones she'd read recently so it didn't work. She must have been really out of it when she packed.

She decided to sleep even if it hadn't worked the last time. She only needed a short break from thinking about Theopolis. No one remembered them. Some of the ones who stayed did so hoping they could save Theopolis. They wanted a brighter future. The worst part was knowing the problem was that the atmosphere couldn't support sentient life.

She couldn't understand how this happened. What had they done to deserve such a calamity? She might never know and even if someone did find out what caused it; who would be around to care? Would anyone ever discover what happened to Theopolis?

She'd felt such fear earlier and she wondered if anyone else ever had to endure the silent, creeping Menace. She'd wanted nothing more than to escape. She wasn't afraid for herself as she'd likely never have to return there. She was afraid for all those who might stumble into that Realm and become trapped there. Would they be able to escape? She tried to avoid the thoughts racing through her mind.

Perhaps the Cousins and Merrick would be able to help her with both problems. She knew they'd focus on helping her deal with what she'd learned on her recent Travels. But she also needed help making sure no one else went through what she did.

Suddenly she was looking at dinner and wondering how far they'd gone. She wasn't sure where they were or who was hosting the reunion this time. Soon she'd be able to stop wondering what would happen when she confessed to her Cousins. She'd get caught with secrets as soon as the adults left them alone to play. Sure the Cousins were nice but they wouldn't let her keep secrets that caused more harm than good. She barely noticed when she drifted off once more.

She woke to the night sky. She hoped she'd one day live in a bedroom painted with constellations covering the walls and ceiling. There was something so comforting about the vastness of the star-studded sky. She wished she could stare at the stars forever.

Finally, the car came to a halt in front of her grandparents' house. She staggered to the door. Dad knocked and Grandpa ushered us to our rooms. We were in the same places we'd been the year before and the other bunk beds were occupied. The rooms were split with boys in one room and girls in another even though we usually found ourselves camped out in the living room. Luckily they were all asleep. Aislinn stumbled over to the open bunk and plopped herself down before falling asleep again. She must have been more tired than she suspected because she didn't Travel.

9.
Alex

"Does anyone know what's up with the adults? Grandma and Grandpa have been acting differently. Haley and I overheard them telling the adults to keep an eye on you and Aislinn." Demetrius said running his hand through his afro.

"Aislinn needs help. She's been having horrible dreams." Alex said.

"You have your parents freaked out enough to ask Grandma, Grandpa, and the rest of the adults for help over a couple bad dreams?" Haley asked incredulously. Demetrius glared at him. "What's so terrible about a couple of dreams," Haley asked, failing to keep the derision out of his voice.

Alex looked at Demetrius before speaking. "Aislinn Travels to other worlds in her dreams and the last two were terrifying. She found an interactive globe showing a planet called Theopolis. When she asked what the place looked like now it showed a desolate, hostile environment. She asked what happened and saw the death of the planet as its atmosphere became unbreathable. She saw the people there fleeing, but not all could escape, and some chose to stay in the hopes of fixing the planet's atmosphere. Their best and brightest minds were killed and she saw it happen." Alex said, trying not to cry.

"Alex. I hate to ask but what happened in the other dream-world?" Demetrius asked as gently as he could.

"She went to another world soon after. She'd been having nightmares so we did our best to keep her distracted throughout the day. But, once she fell asleep there was nothing we could do. She was trapped there. Our parents came in to check on her and found her unresponsive. When I could, I called a Traveler hoping they could help. If they hadn't appeared she might not have been able to return." He sobbed.

Demetrius stared at his cousin in horror before moving to hug him. Demetrius, Thackery, and Zinnia had inherited their dark complexion and curls from their dad, Uncle Ferdinand.

Thackery and Zinnia hugged Aislinn and she almost seemed to disappear beneath their curls. Demetrius let go of Alex once he stopped crying. The cousins looked at each other and nodded in agreement.

"I used to dream all the time. I remember being so excited to go to sleep and have all kinds of amazing adventures. I was nine when I realized other people don't dream like I do. I spent another couple of months trying my best to ignore that fact. Eventually, Haley found out

I was searching for a way to enter my dreams permanently. He told me I was needed here and my family would miss me. He tried to explain that dreams weren't always safe and running to them wouldn't make things better. After all, no world is perfect." Demetrius said.

Zinnia looked up at her older brother and with tears in her eyes pleaded. "Don't leave me. I love you too much for you to go. Promise." She begged. She hugged him refusing to let go and started to cry. When Thackery tried to make her let go of their older brother she cried harder prompting Demetrius to pick her up and make simple shushing sounds. She finally stopped sobbing but when her brother tried to put her down she screamed and held him tighter.

"I understand you're concerned but I'm fine. This was years ago. If you really feel I need help I promise to talk to someone after we've dealt with the other things going on. However, with Aislinn having night terrors so severe she becomes comatose this takes a backseat." Demetrius insisted.

Finally, the hugging and susurrus of concerns diminished. The cousins argued about who should explain next. After a short vote, Thackery was chosen.

Thackery pushed his brown curls out of his eyes and began to fidget under Haley's gaze. Thackery lifted his head, squared his shoulders, and spoke with a confidence Alex didn't know he had. "Is there anyone here who doesn't know what it means to be a Traveler?" Zinnia raised her hand.

"Travelers are people who Travel to other worlds. The easiest methods are dreaming or daydreaming. Traveling through dreams is preferable but Traveling through daydreams is more common. Everyone who Travels has to use a ritual to do so. However, the ritual varies from person to person. All worlds are connected and collectively they're called the Shadow Realms. The ability to Travel is something everyone has. Children Travel until they forget how or decide not to. People who Travel longer tend to be creative, tolerant, and capable of looking at things in new ways. That being said, there are good and bad Travelers just like there are good and bad people." Thackery said, taking a breath.

"Great but how is this going to help Aislinn. We already know things aren't perfect in the Shadow Realms. I just want to save my sister's life. The rest of it's unnecessary. How are we going to fix this?" Alex asked impatiently.

"I know you're stressed but yelling at me won't solve anything," Thackery said.

"I don't want to fight. I've been so stressed I forgot our moms call each other about everything. I hate knowing this is an enemy I can't fight. I'm supposed to take care of Aislinn. I feel like I'm failing her and I can't afford to fail." Alex said struggling to hold back tears he walked over and began hugging Aislinn.

"What have you already tried to do to solve things?" Seeing the guilty look on Alex's face which no doubt matched the one on

Aislinn's he explained. "I don't care about getting you in trouble with the adults. I don't even care about what you've been up to in the Shadow Realms. I only want to know what you've done to try and stop the nightmares. If we don't know what you've tried we'll waste time. This is big; big enough we can't afford to keep secrets. I know you're hiding something and since it could result in you being harmed we need to know what it is." Thackery said.

Alex shuddered when the piercing gaze of his usually peaceful cousin showed traces of leashed anger. "I'm sorry Aislinn. I'm not going to be able to hide anything. I could've kept some things secret if I'd been asked by anyone else. I just never imagined Thackery would be the one to interrogate me." He would've continued to explain but the glare on Thackery's face and the offended looks on everyone else's made him stop and try to compose himself.

"I met a Traveler before I began Traveling. They said their name was Merrick and told me I could play a game where I'd get to Travel to other Realms. They said I could go to a place called the Shadow Realms. Merrick said it was the name of the interconnected worlds I could Travel to. I asked them how many worlds there were. They said there were an infinite amount of worlds and tried to explain something about the multiverse but I was four and didn't care. Merrick gave me a ritual to follow and became my 'imaginary friend'. I told everyone about Merrick. It's not my fault no one believed me. Eventually, Merrick said I no longer needed to be taught but gave me a way to contact them just in case. I called Merrick after Aislinn's second night terror. They brought her home and told me if she'd been gone any longer she'd be dead. I was hoping I could call them again to see if they could help. It might not help but it can't hurt." Alex said with a sigh.

Everyone present stared at him in confusion. Zinnia recovered first and her suggestion shocked Alex. "We should nest tonight. Thackeray should go with me to ask in case the cuteness isn't enough to convince the adults." Zinnia said with a grin.

10.
Thackery

Thackery and Zinnia walked toward where the adults were gathered hand in hand before knocking on the door to the living room. When they were invited in Zinnia let go of Thackery's hand and walked over to Talia. "Mommy, I's scawed to sleep by myselfs. Can I sleeps with the cousins? If we nests I might not need a nightlight. It'll help Aislinn and Alex too. They looked likes they were gonna cwys today. I wants to helps them and since I asked they won't feel bads." She added.

Thackery wanted to facepalm. Zinnia was laying it on way too thick. He hated when she lisped to get her way. She only did it when she wanted something. He didn't understand why no one ever stopped her. They must know she was doing it on purpose. She was five years old she didn't need to talk like a three-year-old.

The adults seemed conflicted and when it seemed like they'd say no Zinnia started pouting and making her eyes real big and starting to tear up. "Pweeze!" Zinnia begged.

Thackery couldn't resist letting out a sigh. His mom gave him a stern look with her brown eyes and he did his best to keep quiet while he waited for a decision.

The adults looked at each other before replying "Yes, but we do have a few rules. I want you to get everyone so I only have to explain it once." Talia insisted.

Thackery stayed put and waited while Zinnia went to get everyone. He did his best not to fidget but it was hard with all of the adults looking at him. He knew he should've gone with her. He forgot how much he hated being the center of attention.

A few minutes later the kids were all present and looking nervous as the adults stared at them stone-faced. Alex nudged Haley, reminding him to speak for them. "What's this about? Zinnia forgot to tell us anything." Haley said.

Ferdinand looked at his wife Talia before speaking. "Zinnia asked if she could nest with everyone tonight. But first, everyone needs to agree to some ground rules. Bedtime's extended by half an hour tonight. We will check on you periodically. Someone needs to get an adult if anything happens. Haley, you and Demetrius will be in charge. Do you think you can handle that?" He asked.

Haley looked at Demetrius and they nodded.

The rest of the day passed in a blur and before they knew it they were setting out the blankets and pillows that would make up the nest. Zinnia and Aislinn would enter first and be placed near each other.

Alex took up residence on Aislinn's other side and Aislinn cuddled up to him sleepily. Haley and Demetrius had the latest bedtime but entered the nest early.

11.
Aislinn

Aislinn had just settled down to sleep when she felt the familiar ritual occurring. Curious and strangely unafraid she closed her eyes. 'Help me do what's necessary. Help me see what I must and learn what must be learned.' She didn't know if she could handle another night terror. She entered a place with hundreds of orbs. She felt compelled to pick them up but resisted. She searched for the perfect orb. She found a beautiful orb and picked it up. It seemed to pulse and she thought she should be afraid but instead, she smiled and looked at the shelf. There were instructions printed on it and she wondered why she hadn't noticed them before. She spoke a single word and everything changed. "Activate."

The orb seemed to grow or maybe she shrunk she didn't know. Suddenly she realized the orb represented a planet. She felt she should recognize the process but instead waited for it to grow enough for her to step onto the surface. The planet was beautiful and teeming with life. It seemed familiar. The animals were friendly and she saw people wandering around. Before she could speak everything changed. The air grew dark and a sticky raspberry-blue fog began to seep in. The flying creatures became stuck in it and the creatures it touched began to die.

It moved slowly and she watched paralyzed as she realized she was watching Theopolis die again. She tried to warn people. No one could hear her and she realized she was only a bystander. She wouldn't be allowed to help them. She'd never felt so helpless. She tried to leave but she couldn't. She'd have to see it through to the inevitable end.

Her heart sank as she observed her worst fears becoming reality. She felt such mental anguish it began to cause physical pain as she started to keen. She knew she should be worried about her physical body but she wasn't. She was almost afraid to find out why she kept seeing this. There must be some reason she was unable to quit viewing these atrocities.

She tried to flee from the images and began to weep. Watching them die or flee for their lives destroyed her. The world of Theopolis was dying and she felt she'd been there for weeks watching them attempt to find a solution. Even after many of the people there had left the planet she still couldn't leave. She watched the scientists and skeptics stay and saw many of them die. A few scientists were smart enough to use suspended animation or cryogenics and aimed themselves at a nearby colony. They did so in the hopes of being woken up when the danger was gone. The fear continued and she remained paralyzed with anxiety and overloaded empathy.

12.
Thackery

Thackery woke to chaos. Alex was sobbing as he tried desperately to wake Aislinn. Thackery didn't know what to do. He wanted to help, but he didn't know how. Luckily his brother Demetrius turned to him.

Demetrius looked at him and spoke. "Thackery, I need you to take Zinnia to mom and dad. Aislinn's having a night terror and she's been shaking for half an hour without waking. I don't think we're qualified to handle this. Try not to wake Zin. She doesn't need to see this."

Thackery nodded and hugged his brother before slowly picking up Zinnia. If Zinnia saw Aislinn this terrified she'd get scared. He decided to stop thinking and get to the adults as quickly as he could without waking Zinnia. He'd knocked over a picture frame but barely noticed. It seemed like it took forever to get to his parents. He stopped at the door and knocked softly grateful Zinnia had stayed asleep.

His mom Talia opened the door sleepily.

Thackery wanted to explain what was going on but first he needed to place Zinnia somewhere safe. "Mom, can I put Zinnia down with you and Dad? I need to get everyone." He explained.

Talia opened the door wider. "What happened?" His mom asked.

"Dee sent me to get the adults. Aislinn's shaking and whimpering but she won't wake up. Dee didn't want Zinnia to see her. Alex is freaking out and we need help. I'm scared mom. You have to help!" Thackery begged trying to fight back the fear threatening to make him stutter. He looked up at his mom with tears in his eyes.

His mom reached out to hold him close for a moment. "Thackery, I'm going to wake up your dad and leave Zinnia with him. When that's done I'll go with you to get the rest of the adults and we'll figure out what to do from there." His mom said.

Talia grabbed a sweater and put it on along with her slippers. She woke her husband and handed him Zinnia. "Honey I need you to watch Zinnia. Something's wrong with the kids. I'm going to help. I'll explain later." She said while Thackery watched her kiss his dad and hand over Zinnia.

They quickly arrived at Rosemary and Levi's doorway and knocked loudly. Uncle Levi answered the door. He looked confused but invited them in. Uncle Levi sat down and raised an eyebrow.

Thackery's mom looked at Uncle Levi and drew in a deep breath before speaking "Thackery woke me insisting I take Zinnia so he could get the rest of the adults. He told me Aislinn was having a night terror and wouldn't wake up. Alex is freaking out. Demetrius sent Thackery to get help. I don't know how long this has been going on. If you send Rosemary to get Aislinn's parents we can get mom and dad." She suggested.

Levi shook his hair out of his eyes. "I'll wake Rosemary. Will you wait a few minutes for me?" He asked.

A few minutes later Rosemary ran out of the room. Thackery and his mom went to wake his grandparents while the adults rallied everyone else. They made it to his grandparents' room and knocked. His grandma opened the door.

"What do you need?" Grandma Smith asked.

"Aislinn's having a nightmare, Alex is crying, we need help. They're in the living room. Come quick." Thackery said as quickly as he could. His grandma left him momentarily and came back with his Grandpa.

"Let's go," Grandpa said as they rushed to the living room.

When they arrived Grandma and Grandpa Smith proceeded to take charge. "Rosemary, I want you to take Thackery to your room to calm down. He doesn't need to see this. Paisley, you take Demetrius and Haley to see if they know how this started. Talia, Levi I want you to try and help Alex calm down. The rest of you focus on helping Aislinn. Her night terrors are worse than we expected and if things don't improve she needs to see a doctor." Grandpa insisted.

Thackery followed Rosemary out of the room trying not to feel guilty about being glad to escape. Looking up at his aunt he realized staying with her might be as much for her benefit as his. She looked devastated and he reached up to hold her hand. Maybe this time he could help her instead of causing her pain.

13.
Alex

Alex looked at his sister and decided to do what he could to help. Unlike Aislinn, he knew what could happen if one stayed too long in the Shadow Realms. He would do whatever it took to prevent that fate.

He started the ritual and left his body. He thought of finding his sister and nothing else. *Lead me to her,* he thought, trying with all his might to force himself to Travel to her. He wished he'd had the foresight to ask her to stay in the safer Realms. Oh well, hindsight is twenty-twenty.

For once he saw nothing. He moved forward until he saw a light in the distance. He was too far away to see it properly, so he moved closer. When his eyes adjusted he saw Theopolis being destroyed repeatedly, a never-ending cycle of destruction and planetary extinction.

He felt horrified when he realized his sister was watching this. He'd come here to find her and he certainly wouldn't have chosen to watch this. But why would Aislinn be watching this? As soon as she realized what was happening she should have Traveled home. He hoped she wasn't trapped again like last time.

Alex kept moving forward and saw the violet glow that he recognized as a Traveler hovering in the void. As he approached he realized it was his sister and he began to run toward her. Aislinn stood like a statue as she wept. Alex reached her and hugged her hard as he struggled to find a solution. He hated seeing his vibrant sister reduced to this.

It was only then that he remembered the words of the oldest Traveler he'd ever encountered. They'd seen so many things that newcomers often mistook them for an oracle. It didn't help that their advice and predictions were always on target. Thinking about it though pretending not to have seer powers might be helpful for an oracle. After all, who's going to kidnap someone who doesn't have powers just to get good advice? "Should you have a great need or encounter a Traveler in dire straits call for the Wise Ones who call themselves 'Observers'." It hadn't been much help at the time but now it might save his sister's life.

Thinking quickly he decided to do this with ceremony. "Wise Ones, I ask that ye come forth and aid me. I have found a Traveling youngling in dire straits. I fear the Traveler's life may be at risk, for they have been gone overlong from their homeworld. This one was sent to bring the child home. The child grows weak and knows me not despite our familial relation. Please I beg thee to come and give aid, lest a youngling be lost forever." He pleaded hoping it would work.

When it appeared no one was coming and he felt himself growing weak as well he sent one last plea. "Please give aid. I am fading and I fear my family may lose two younglings tonight. If we die, the Shadow Realms will lose more than two Travelers. All of my cousins will know no one cared enough to help us and they will cease to Travel as well. Do you really want to lose an entire lineage of Travelers?" He asked, trying to stay conscious. He wasn't sure what would happen if he lost consciousness in the Shadow Realms but he didn't want to find out.

Finally, he heard the sound he'd been waiting for. The Observers chose to intervene. The first one was the largest of the three. He tried to picture what they looked like and when he found himself unable to he realized they were wearing image distorters. He was both relieved and angered when he realized Merrick was not among them. The largest one appeared to be female but they were most likely all shapeshifters. Unable to remember the proper procedure for dealing with shapeshifters or Observers he stuck to Traveler etiquette.

"Greetings Traveler. I wish the circumstances of our meeting had been better. We had hoped not to interfere. We wished to see how you would handle the challenges you've been given. I recommend not threatening us again. We won't be as understanding should it happen again." The largest one said.

Alex looked at the group and spoke hoping they wouldn't take any offense. "Greetings Observers. I thank you for coming to our aid. I too wish we'd met under better circumstances but cannot bring myself to regret you saving my sibling's life." Alex said intentionally leaving off names and genders until they'd mentioned what they'd like to be called. He must have remembered more about shapeshifter etiquette than he'd thought.

"Would you mind informing me of what you'd like to be called? I don't mean to be rude, I'd just like to know who I'm addressing. It would also make it easier for my sibling and I to thank you for saving our lives." He said hoping they'd take it in the spirit in which it was intended. He was banking on his age saving him in case they took offense to his question.

"Wise words young traveler. Given the severity of the situation, I shall grant you leave to speak informally. Don't make me regret giving you said privilege." The largest observer said in a soft voice threaded with steel. "Our names are unpronounceable to you but we shall introduce ourselves. My name is Geth, the smallest one is my apprentice Xelleth and the surly-looking one over there is Nithkin. Don't pay any attention to Nithkin. That one is merely angry that they had to leave the comforts of home. Nithkin hates to travel." Geth snickered before continuing. "Both Nithkin and Xelleth are younglings by our standards though Xelleth is the older of the two. If they start bickering or fighting let me know and I'll sort it out." Geth said with a smile.

He took a moment to calm down before replying. "My name is Alex and this is Aislinn. As you can see Aislinn is a youngling and still requires protection. As the eldest child, it is my responsibility to help. Since my parents are unable to Travel it's up to me to fix this. I'm not leaving till Aislinn's safe." He growled before realizing he should be nicer. "I'm sorry for my rudeness, I'm just frightened. I don't want Aislinn to die," he said.

He was only now realizing how hard it was to speak without using gendered pronouns. Merrick would be so disappointed in him. This kind of speech had been drilled into him time and time again. Yet, here he was blundering around like a three-year-old. If they found out Merrick was the one who'd mentored him they'd never forgive his rudeness. He should have paid more attention to his lessons. He hadn't believed Merrick when they said good manners might save his life.

Alex looked at Aislinn and wondered what it would take to save her. The Observers did their best to awaken Aislinn using the simplest methods. When this failed they began attempting the more complicated methods of waking a Traveler. Deciding to avoid the slower methods in favor of faster ones they started to discuss the procedure. As they prepared to pull out the big guns they elected Geth the spokesperson. Geth hemmed and hawed before approaching Alex once more.

"Is there a Traveler Aislinn knows who might be able to help them return to their body? I fear we might need reinforcements and you are weakened enough that we don't feel comfortable letting you help." Geth muttered shifting around as if speaking the words made them physically ill. Finally, Geth managed to get a grip and resumed speaking this time in a stern tone as opposed to the awkward one from before. "We don't need two younglings in danger of dying. You are not going to interfere. Should you do so, the other youngling may die. Such a death would be senseless and serve no purpose. Do you understand?" Geth growled.

"Aislinn knows a lot of Travelers, all my cousins Travel. But the only Traveler Aislinn knows that might be capable of helping is a shapeshifter that goes by Merrick who I suspect is also an Observer." Alex said hoping they wouldn't be too angry.

Geth looked at Alex and appeared to be contemplating something. "I am aware of the one who goes by Merrick. We have helped each other in the past. As to your speculations about whether or not they are an Observer, that is something you'll have to take up with them." Geth said giving Alex a sinister grin. "I will call Merrick and have them help us with this pre-dic-a-ment," Geth said.

Geth walked away with Xelleth and Nithkin as they discussed how to summon Merrick. At least that's what Alex assumed they were discussing as they moved out of earshot. Geth walked back bringing an excited Xelleth and a grumbling Nithkin. "The one you call

Merrick is coming but before Merrick does." Geth paused before continuing. "There's something you should know about Aislinn." Here Geth tried to smile; it came out more like a grimace.

At this point Xelleth interrupted. "Oh, for the sake of the Shadow Realms. They'll never learn what they need to know if you keep hemming and hawing. There is a group of Observers that think Aislinn is the Prophecy Child. Some of them may have been less careful with the youngling's safety than we'd like. The prophecy about the Traveler who will save Theopolis was recorded eons ago. In all that time Aislinn is the only one to come close enough to hear the prophecy. This led them to believe that Aislinn must be the Prophecy Child. I'm so excited I've never met a Chosen One before."

Alex couldn't help but interject hoping no one was offended. "I've heard the Prophecy. I've even seen Theopolis. If this group was wrong about that then who's to say they aren't wrong about who the Chosen One is. Aislinn is only seven. That's much too young to be saving worlds, especially without help!" Alex said glaring at them as if daring them to say something. Sensing that this might not be enough he pulled out his trump card.

"Even if Aislinn is the Prophecy Child and I'm not saying Aislinn is, there is no way Aislinn is going to save Theopolis alone. Nothing in the Prophecy says that the Chosen One can't have help. What kind of people make a seven-year-old solve their problems without even offering encouragement?" Alex asked.

Xelleth was so shocked that the distortion field fluctuated for a second revealing an electric purple jaw dropping a foot. "But the Observers are never wrong. If they say no one else heard the Prophecy then nobody else heard it." Xelleth stammered.

"Well, they were wrong this time. I snuck into the Observer's station and played the footage of Aislinn finding Theopolis and the Prophecy. That's how I know nothing says the Chosen One must save Theopolis alone." Alex snarled.

Finally, Geth stepped in when it seemed like Alex and Xelleth might come to blows. "Now, now children. Everyone makes mistakes. We just have to decide what to do about them. Alex, did you really trespass in the Observer's station?"

Alex nodded not trusting his voice to remain steady in the face of such a fearsome glare. "It's impossible to lie to a Traveler without being caught so Alex must have heard the prophecy. That being said, we need to get back to solving the problem of how to help young Aislinn." Geth said.

Alex breathed a sigh of relief when Merrick arrived. His mentor would know what to do. "Alex I need you to come with me. I believe I've found the source of Aislinn's Traveling problems. It appears your new friends know what happened. I think it might be their fault. I just wish I knew why. What possible motive could they have?" Merrick asked in a whisper.

"Why didn't you tell me the Observers were the reason Aislinn's been having trouble Traveling?" Merrick demanded glaring at the three unnamed Observers. Of the three; the smallest appeared horrified, the middle one looked confused and the largest one was unfazed. The big one was in on it.

Alex couldn't take it anymore, he had to know. "Were you ever going to help us or was it all part of some scheme? I won't let you make my sibling into a weapon! I don't care if you guys need a hero. Killing Aislinn will not endear you to my family. You need to fix this and if you don't agree to do so right now and cease interfering" Alex cut himself off. "I'll do my best to keep Aislinn as far away from you as possible even if that means you never receive your precious Prophecy Child!" Alex yelled.

"If you don't fix this right now I'm calling in the Council. I've got no problem filing charges. Let's go over them right now. We have two counts of child endangerment. Multiple counts of breaking the Traveler's Code. Three counts of attempted murder of a youngling. One count of treason against the Shadow Realms. Two counts of attempted murder of an apprentice. Two counts of breaking the treatise between the Observers and Travelers. Multiple counts of false imprisonment of a youngling and a final count of attempted Xenocide. What do you think the Council will have to say about that?" Merrick asked, baring their teeth.

Geth appeared to get very uncomfortable the longer Merrick listed things. "Fine, I'll fix this. I promise to leave Aislinn alone and not interfere with the youngling's Travels. However, I would like two things in return. One; please don't send me to the Council and two; I would like for Aislinn to begin training as the Prophecy Child." Geth asked the tiniest bit of hope leaching into their voice.

"I will take you to the Council. They'll find the rest of your crew. There's no way you came up with this by yourself." Geth glared at Merrick. "As for Aislinn receiving training to become the Prophecy Child; that will never happen. Aislinn has agreed to be my apprentice. Training to become something that might be impossible would detract from their real studies. I suspect Aislinn isn't the Chosen One but by forcing the issue you may have alienated the real Chosen One." Merrick sneered.

Alex smiled at the being he'd be apprenticing under and was imminently grateful he'd thought to ask Merrick to apprentice his sister as well. He'd had no idea what protections it offered when he asked. Which, now that he thought about it might have been why Merrick agreed.

His sister would likely be safe at home soon. With those cheerful thoughts in mind, he began to plan out what to say to his folks. The cousins would of course be told the truth but that still left him with the question of what to say to the adults; especially his parents.

Alex watched as Geth reluctantly called for assistance. He saw Geth pale when three Observers arrived and seven Council members followed right behind. The Council members walked toward Geth and brought out the glowing restraints. The smallest Council member walked toward Geth.

"The being calling itself Geth is hereby being held by the Council for crimes of treason, breaking the Traveler's Code, crimes against younglings, harming apprentices, attempted Xenocide, attempted murder, and other crimes yet to be determined. I do not recommend Shape-shifting or trying to contact your friends. We've captured most of them already. Zilkin grab Xelleth would you? The Council doesn't know if they're involved but since Xelleth is Geth's apprentice the youngling may know something." The Council member said with a vicious smirk.

The Council member then walked over to Nithkin and smiled warmly. "Nithkin, for your undercover work we hereby grant you apprentice status. This gives you the right to train for a seat on the Council when you are older pending a review of course. We are very proud of your work here. That being said, we recommend you train as a shapeshifter before determining your future career. Live well young one." The council member said as kind to Nithkin as they were cruel to Geth.

Alex watched this all unfold with a confused look. He understood that Geth got arrested for what sounded like a ton of horrifying crimes; mostly against children. Nithkin was undercover and helped uncover the plot the rogue group of Observers cooked up. He knew they found his sister's plight hard to handle but that was no excuse for letting things deteriorate.

Just as he began searching for his cousins he heard his sister whimper. He turned to her startled. They'd been here for quite some time and in all that time she hadn't moved or made a sound, just let tears roll down her face. This was progress but for good or ill he didn't know.

Alex rushed to her side and held her hand. "It's okay to come home. no one will be mad at you. We just want you to be okay. Please, come home. Our family needs you. Please, Aislinn, I'm begging you to come back. I don't want to lose you." Alex whispered hoping it would help. He needed her to be okay. He couldn't handle the thought of his sister dying. Shaking his head to clear it of the painful thoughts he reached out and grabbed her hand.

Without being so close Alex would never have heard her whispered words. "Alex, I'm lost. Alex." She whispered. Only the knowledge that his sister needed him to be brave kept him from crying.

"Aislinn's asking me to find her," Alex yelled, unwilling to move. With those words, the Council members who weren't guarding Geth and Xelleth hurried over with Merrick and Nithkin.

"Are you sure Aislinn spoke?" Nithkin asked. "Aislinn hasn't made a sound yet and no one's done anything to help the youngling. Why wouldn't Aislinn have spoken earlier if they were able to ask for help?" Nithkin asked.

"Nithkin, I respect that you're wanting us to be realistic but the child is facing losing a younger sibling. A little tact wouldn't go amiss. This is why you've never advanced in the ranks and why despite your age none of the Masters or Mentors will take you as an apprentice. Your social skills are horrendous. I doubt you will ever become a Council member if this is how you treat those below you in power. You are an ambassador for the shapeshifters and you're making us look bad. What if Alex had never met another shapeshifter and you were all the child had to go on? What would Alex think of our race? I do not appreciate the disrespect you are showing my apprentices. I will not warn you again. Do I make myself clear child?" Merrick asked, baring their teeth.

Nithkin took a step back unable to hide their fear of Merrick.

Merrick walked toward Aislinn. All Alex could do was hope and watch with bated breath as Merrick reached his sister; it seemed to take hours. "Aislinn, I need you to listen to the sound of my voice. Can you do that for me?" Merrick asked.

"Alex is here with me. Do you think you can come back? You're safe here. I won't let anyone hurt you." Merrick said, trying to soothe Aislinn's fears.

"We'll get through this. You'll see. The Cousins will help us. You don't have to do this alone. We're here now. All you have to do is trust us." Alex said, waiting for Aislinn to come back to him. He held her vowing that he'd do everything in his power to ensure she was never hurt like this again. Slowly Aislinn sank into his embrace.

"Come on kiddo. It's time to go home. Everyone's waiting for you. You'll see. Mom and dad won't let you out of their sight after this." With those words, Alex tightened his hold on her before looking at Merrick to let them know he was taking her home. Normally he'd wait 'til things cleared up but he didn't know how long they'd been gone. For all he knew, they were en route to a hospital by now.

"Thank you, Merrick! I look forward to seeing you again without the near-death experiences and psychological trauma." Alex said before starting the ritual to return home.

14.
Aislinn

"You saved me," Aislinn whispered as their parents turned to her. Suddenly all eyes were on her.

"Oh, honey. Everything's fine. It was just a dream." Her mom insisted. She could hear the pain in her mother's voice.

"Dad. Is Aislinn gonna be okay?" Alex asked in a shaky voice.

Her dad turned to him. "She'll be fine now. You'll see. She's gonna get through this and we're gonna help her." He said, pulling Alex into a tight hug.

Alex walked toward her. He reached over and hugged her. Alex whispered in her ear. "I'm going to do everything I can to bring you back. I promise. I love you." She didn't say anything, just burrowed into his chest and hugged him back.

The hug ended and Alex stepped back. "You know you can come to me with anything don't you?" He asked.

"I know." She whispered.

Their mom gasped. "I love seeing you two get along so well. If I'd known you were going to be this nice to each other I'd have gotten it on video. That way the next time you fight I can prove that you do love each other."

"Moooom."

"Don't *moooom'* me, young man. If I want photographic evidence that you two love each other that's my prerogative. As your mother I prefer the two of you to get along. Besides I'm sure there are some lovely photos of you acting like a dork I could show your friends." She said with a smirk.

Aislinn giggled. "I wouldn't tempt fate. I have pictures of you too." With that parting shot, Aislinn reddened and the giggles stopped.

Their dad walked in seeing Aislinn's red face and Alex looking at the ground while his wife smirked. "Did I miss something?"

"Alex asked Aislinn if she knew she could come to him with anything. She said yes. It was so cute. I wish I'd had a video and I mentioned it aloud. So Alex started whining and I threatened to show his friends photos of him being a dork. Aislinn laughed at him and I reminded her that I had photos of her too. Then you walked in."

"Awww. I missed out on a chance to threaten the kids with all the photos we've collected." He pouted.

"Don't worry hon. I'm sure you have some pictures you could show that I wouldn't think to use to embarrass the kids."

"That's true. There's always pictures of Alex at the princess tea party and Aislinn holding onto the dragon she sleeps with." Their dad said with a devious grin.

"Ooooh. I'd forgotten about those. See I told you there'd be cards for you to play. Besides, it's more fun to embarrass them together." Their parents cackled for a few minutes.

"We're glad you two are getting along so well. You're going to be spending a lot more time together. We've decided to enroll you in homeschool." His dad said, waiting to see their reactions.

"Okay." They chorused with no inflection.

"I was expecting more of a reaction."

"Too tired," Alex said.

Their parents started laughing. "If that's the case you should probably try and get some sleep." Her mom said before herding them back to the nest in the living room.

"Time for bed. Tomorrow's gonna be a long day." The adults said turning out the lights and walking away.

"We'll talk tomorrow," Alex said before curling up and trying to sleep.

"I'm not going anywhere. I've had enough excitement for one night." Aislinn promised.

15.
Thackery

"Have you seen Alex?" Aislinn asked.

"Not yet. I thought he'd be with you. Especially after last night." Thackery replied.

"I haven't seen him since breakfast. He finished before I did and left. He didn't even bother to wash his dishes. Just stuck them in the sink and walked away. Ugh. Why does he have to be so lazy?" Aislinn complained.

Thackery saw the look in her eyes and decided not to stick around. "I hope you find him. See you later. Bye." He yelled over his shoulder before looking for someone to hang out with. Normally he'd look for Alex but he didn't want to get between the siblings when they fought.

There had to be something he could do. Maybe Zinnia would let him play with her. His face fell. Zinnia would be cuddling up to Aunt Rosemary trying to cheer her up. Suddenly he saw Aunt Paisley walking around scribbling in a notebook. Her purple hair was up in its customary bun.

"Auntie Paisley. Can I talk to you for a minute?" He asked wondering if she'd resent his intrusion.

"What's up Ree?" She asked, tucking her notebook away in one of her many pockets.

"Everybody's busy and I was hoping you could help me figure out what I could do for entertainment." He said peering up at her shyly.

"Sure. I was just adding some things to my sketchbook. Wanna help me decide what to paint?" She asked.

"What if I mess up?" Thackery asked.

"Art isn't something you can mess up silly. There's no right or wrong way to do it. It just is." Paisley assured him.

"But how will I help you figure out what to paint?" Thackery asked, cocking his head like a spaniel.

"We're going to go for a walk and anytime you see something interesting or think of something you'd like to see a picture of you'll tell me and I'll make a note in my sketchbook. When we get back to this spot we'll look through my notes and decide from there." Paisley suggested.

"Okay."

"Are you ready Ree? We'll need to pay very close attention to our surroundings so we don't miss anything."

"I'm ready," Thackery said with a smile.

"Great. Where should we look first?" Paisley asked.

"That depends on what kind of painting you want to make. There's a spooky tree that looks like it's going to grab you in that direction." Thackery said pointing toward the direction Paisley came from.

"No thanks. I've seen that tree and I don't want to imagine it grabbing anyone. I think I'd rather paint something cheerful."

"The garden has a spot that looks like a fairy playground. Would that work?" Thackery asked hoping she wouldn't tell anyone he said that. He'd talked to Haley about it once and been teased for weeks. He hated the blond menace not that he was allowed to call Haley that but what no-one knew wouldn't get him in trouble.

"That's perfect. Why don't we head over there and you point out anything else you think would make a good picture. Who knows. You might be able to come up with a series of paintings." Paisley teased.

"But I'm not an artist; not like you and Uncle Kane." Thackery protested.

"Au contraire, Mon, Frere. You came up with the idea of what to paint. If you weren't an artist you wouldn't have done that. That makes you an artist." Paisley insisted.

"But I'm not creative," Thackery said looking at his shoes.

"Are too. You know what you want to make and the ideas pop into your head uninvited. Now you just have to practice making the ideas reality."

"Is that what you and Uncle Kane do?" Thackery asked.

"Sure. That part can be taught but what you just did can't. That knack for looking at something and seeing its potential is innate."

"What's innate mean?" Thackery asked.

"It's what you're born with. You can't be a good artist without creativity and imagination. Anyone can recreate a picture of something beautiful if they practice enough but making something that didn't exist before takes something extra and you have that." She said with a smile.

"I don't think so. I'm nothing special. I'm just Thackery." He said kicking a rock out of his way.

"Silly Ree. You're an artist. You'll see. One day you'll get a brilliant idea and make it come to life. It won't be perfect and you'll get frustrated when it doesn't come out like you wanted, but eventually, you'll make something else. Then one day you'll wake up and realize that you're a writer or a painter or a sculptor and you'll remember me telling you you were an artist." Paisley declared as if it was obvious.

"I don't think anyone cares what ideas I have," Thackery muttered.

"What did you just say?"

"Nothing."

"Don't lie to me," Paisley demanded. "I know you said something and this time you're going to repeat it so that I can hear you."

"I don't want to."

"Thackery Octavian Wallace. You can either tell me what you said or I can talk to your parents about what I think I heard. It's your choice."

"It's not a big deal," Thackery said, hoping she'd let it go.

"It is if you said what I think you said. Now I'm going to give you one last chance to settle this privately."

"I don't think anyone cares what ideas I have. I'm just Thackery. Stupid, useless Thackery." He admitted looking at his shoes.

"What gave you that idea?" Paisley asked.

"I hear it all the time. It's what kids at school used to say. Even Zin's starting to avoid me." Thackery said, trying not to cry.

"What about your brother? Doesn't he spend time with you?" Paisley asked.

"No. He's too busy and his friends don't like hanging around babies." Thackery spat.

"Did he say that to you?" Paisley asked her voice tightening.

"That's just it. He doesn't say anything. His friends say it for him and he lets them. His silence speaks volumes."

"Do you want me to talk to him?"

"No. He'll just end up mad that I tattled on him like a baby."

"Will you at least tell me who called you stupid and useless?" Paisley asked.

"No. He'll get mad and my brother will hate me."

"Did your brother say that?"

"No."

"Did his friends say that in front of him?"

"No. His friends say he's too busy and tell me to go back to the other babies."

"Then who called you stupid and useless?" Paisley queried.

"It doesn't matter."

"It does. You wouldn't have repeated it if you didn't believe them."

"I'm not telling."

"Then I'll have to talk to your parents. They need to know you said this and they're going to ask where you got the idea. If they don't get an answer they'll assume your brother said it and you're covering for him."

"I'm not. He wouldn't say that to me. He might think it but he wouldn't say it." Thackery insisted.

"What makes you think he believes it if he never said it?"

"He has time for everybody except me. He and Haley are practically joined at the hip. He's even reached out to Alex and Aislinn and he only sees them a few times a year."

"Did you tell him you felt left out?"

"No. I got tired of hearing that he didn't have time for me. The only time he comes up to me is to ask me where someone else is or if I've been looking out for Zin." Thackery pouted. "Just because he has no time for me doesn't mean I have no time for Zin. She's my sister too. I don't need to be told to spend time with her."

"I hated being told what to do too. Especially if I was already doing it."

"Just cause Dee is older than me doesn't mean he gets to lecture me. He's not my dad." Thackery insisted.

"Older siblings are weird like that. They usually mean well but sometimes it makes things worse." Paisley said, giving him a knowing look.

"Did you have to deal with that a lot when you were my age?"

"Yeah. It got better as I got older. Finally, I told your Uncle Kane that it made me feel bad."

"Did it help?"

"He backed off and convinced everyone else to as well. He said lecturing me all the time wasn't helping and if it kept up I'd stop trusting them. Afterward, I didn't have any more problems."

"They stopped telling you what to do."

"No. My siblings decided they wouldn't tell me what to do unless it was really important. I stopped hiding things from them which made them happier too. Everybody won." Paisley admitted.

"Oh. Do you think Dee is bugging me because he's worried?" Thackery asked.

"Probably. I think he's worried you don't have a lot of friends and telling you to watch Zin might be his way of making sure you have someone to hang out with."

"Why wouldn't he just say that?" Thackery asked.

"He might be embarrassed or worried about upsetting you."

"If he's worried I don't have friends why can't he just spend time with me?" Thackery asked, clenching his fists.

"I don't know. He might be worried about Zinnia since she's the youngest or he could just like telling you what to do. The only way to find out why he's doing it would be to talk to him." Paisley chided.

"He doesn't listen. I've tried talking to him. It never works. He's too busy to listen."

"Okay. If you don't want to talk to him you don't have to but you're not going to get any answers by sulking."

"I'm not sulking." He whined crossing his arms, his lower lip protruding.

"Sure," Paisley said poking his lip back in. "It just looks like you're sulking and your bottom lip protruding doesn't mean you're pouting."

"Quit mocking me."

"Alright. If you want to sulk you're allowed to but if that lip sticks out again I'm going to poke it." Paisley threatened; wagging her finger at him.

Thackery turned to her. "I thought you wanted to paint?" He retorted.

"No. I wanted to find something to paint and I have. Besides I thought you wanted company." She teased.

"You're right." Thackery let out a sigh and smiled up at her. "Now that you know what you want to paint will you paint it?"

"No. Painting takes time. The light shifts over time, especially outside. Once I start working with actual paint it'll take hours or days to finish."

"So you're done for now?"

"No. I'm going to walk over and make a few rough sketches while I decide what I want for the painting. If the light's really good I might even start a detailed sketch. After that, I'll pack up my sketchbook and come back later to start the underdrawing."

"Oh. I never knew painting was so hard," Thackery admitted, his cheeks stained with embarrassment.

"It is but I wouldn't trade it for anything." A dreamy smile overtook her. "I love what I do and it pays the bills. Not all artists are so lucky."

"Could I buy one of your paintings if I wanted?" Thackery asked.

Paisley paused for a second. "I don't sell to family but if you'd like I can give you one for your birthday. I'll need to clear it with your parents but I don't think they'll mind."

"Thanks, aunt Paisley." Thackery grinned at her.

"No problem. I'm happy to help. Since I'm going to give you a painting in about nine months I think it best if you understand the process behind creating one. We're going to have lots of fun Ree." Paisley insisted.

"What are we going to do?" Thackery asked, bouncing around in excitement.

"Well. The first step is to find you something to wear. I have an old smock you can borrow and I'll talk to your mom about getting you some clothes to paint in. For now, we'll sketch in the garden while you point to the spot I should paint. The rest will have to wait 'til tomorrow."

"Awww."

"Don't worry. We'll have lots to do and one day won't make a lot of difference." Paisley said, smiling at him.

"Alright." Thackery pouted for a second before realizing that Paisley didn't have to teach him about painting. "Did anybody else in the family learn to paint from you?" He asked, brown eyes wide and hopeful.

"No. I learned from your Uncle Kane. A lot of the time people forget that I paint since most of my income is made from making blankets. I promised myself years ago that I would never sell my work to my family. I've made all the kids at least one blanket. The first blanket I attempted was used as a rug when your uncle Levi was a kid. Afterward, it became a tradition to make a custom blanket for all the kids in the family."

"Why was your first blanket used as a rug?" Thackery asked, cocking his head.

"Because it was a terrible blanket. I didn't know anything about sewing or quilting. But, I'd promised to make Levi a blanket. Grandma offered to help me but I refused. In the end, the only thing it was good for was a rug. I was proud of it so I put it in the playroom and made another rug. Eventually, they got good enough to be used as blankets and I gave the first nice one to Levi. Afterward, I made one for everyone, and anytime someone joins the family I make them a blanket. " Paisley smiled as she reminisced.

"That's so cool. Do you remember what you made for my mom?" Thackery asked, bouncing around.

"Yes. I've made her a few. My favorite is a cream-colored blanket with black stripes. I embroidered music notes on it so that it looks like sheet music. I did my best to recreate the first song she learned. It wasn't the first blanket I made for her but I think it's the nicest one I've made for her."

"That must've been hard."

"Not really. She started with Twinkle, Twinkle, Little Star"

"How did you find the sheet music?"

"I went to a music shop and asked. I drew the notes bigger and copied them onto the blanket."

"Did my mom like the blanket?" He asked.

"Yes. I think she still has it."

"When I grow up I wanna be as cool as you." Thackery insisted.

"I'd rather you grow up to be Ree. I'm sure it'll be much easier than trying to be someone else."

"I don't wanna be like anyone else. I wanna be like you."

"You're nine. You've got plenty of time to figure things out."

"I don't need to. You're cool and people like you. I wanna be just like you."

Paisley grabbed Thackery and hugged him. "You're perfect just the way you are Ree."

"Then why doesn't anyone want to spend time with me?" Thackery asked.

"I like you and we've spent all morning together," Paisley assured him.

"You're family, you have to spend time with me."

"That's not true. I chose to spend my morning with you. I could've continued searching for something to paint."

"You were just being polite." Thackery insisted.

"I could've apologized for being busy and continued on my way. I'm not going to continue to let you talk bad about yourself. I like you and I wanted to spend time with you. You can either accept that or we can talk to your parents about where you got the outlandish idea that everyone hates you."

"Please don't tell them. They'll get worried and blame themselves. Besides, there are more important things going on." Thackery insisted.

"What could be more important to parents than their child?" Paisley asked.

"Aunt Rosemary's hurting. Haley's been trying to help her but he doesn't know what's wrong. She bursts into tears and hugs him 'til it hurts. Dee said she's depressed but he doesn't know why. Zinnia helps but sometimes when she thinks nobody's looking she cries when she looks at her. I think something happened to her. Something bad and being around us kids is hard for her. She loves us but we're hurting her and I don't know if we can fix it." Thackery explained.

"You're right that is a big problem and I appreciate you guys trying to help but it's a grown-up problem. I can talk to the other adults about it and we can deal with Rosemary but you still haven't convinced me anything's going on which would keep your parents from helping you."

"They can't fix this. No one can. I just have to get used to people not wanting me around." Thackery insisted.

"If you'd tell me where you got the idea that you're a nuisance I could fix this. You're a great kid. I love you, your parents love you. You don't have to go through this alone."

"Yes, I do," Thackery said, stamping his feet.

"If that's how it's going to be I'll have to resort to drastic measures." With those ominous words, Paisley put down the satchel holding her art supplies, looked at Thackery, and proceeded to hug him.

"Let me go." He shouted.

"Not until you admit that you're loveable."

"No."

"Then I won't let you go." Paisley insisted, hugging him tighter.

"You're insuffrable."

"Where did you even learn that word?" Paisley asked amused at the complaint.

"Mommy said it to daddy when he asked if she wanted another baby."

"Do you think he was serious about wanting another kid?"

"No. Mommy said he didn't want another rugrat running around. He just likes making them. Then she said he was insufferable." Thackery said squirming about.

"Ah. That makes more sense."

"Do you want a baby, Auntie Paisley?" Thackery asked.

"No. I'm perfectly happy being Auntie and you only asked because you hoped I'd be so shocked that I'd let you go. It won't work." Paisley's arms tightened.

Paisley smiled and let him go. Thackery ran off. He didn't know what made her give up on the hugging plan but he wasn't going to stick around to find out.

16.
Aislinn

Aislinn looked around. Everyone seemed too busy to help her. She didn't want to talk to anyone about what was happening to her but being alone made it worse.

She hated lying to her family but she wasn't ready to talk about her dreams. She buried her head in her hands and began to sob. She couldn't get the images out of her head. If she closed her eyes she saw Theopolis. She'd thought it would be okay when she woke up but lately she'd started having nightmares while awake. She'd done her best to hide them but she didn't know how long she could keep it up.

She didn't know how long she'd sobbed when she felt someone staring at her. She looked up to see her uncle Levi watching her.

"Do you want to talk about it?" He asked softly the way he'd speak to a frightened animal.

"N-n-no." Aislinn choked out between sobs.

"Alright. You don't have to say anything but I'm not going to leave you like this. Would you like to hear a story?" Levi asked.

Aislinn nodded. She wasn't sure what he wanted to tell her but it had to be better than sitting here bawling her eyes out.

"Did you know I had nightmares when I was little?" He asked, giving her a look she couldn't decipher.

"N-n-no," Aislinn admitted.

"I had them every night. I'd wake up terrified, unable to go back to sleep. Sometimes I'd scream the house awake. Other times I'd be shaking and sweaty, unable to wake. I kept thinking it'd get better but it didn't. Eventually, I got too scared to go to sleep." Levi said, looking at something she couldn't see.

The shock of his words stopped her tears. "Does it ever get better?" She asked.

Her words brought him back from wherever he'd been. "Sometimes. It depends on the cause. Nightmares usually vanish on their own but night terrors are a different beast."

"What's a night terror?" Aislinn asked.

"It's like a nightmare but worse. You don't stop being scared when you wake up and they tend to last longer. We're still not sure what causes them but they don't go away easily. Some people have them for their whole life, others take meds to deal with them." Levi explained.

"Will my dreams go away?" Aislinn asked, tears welling up.

"I don't know sweetheart. I hope so." He said and she started to sob again. He pulled her close and held her as she wept.

When the tears subsided he looked at her. "Do you want to hear the rest of the story?"

"Yes," Aislinn said.

"I don't know who figured out what was wrong first but everyone decided to help me. Talia looked up how to play lullabies. Paisley decided to make me a blanket to help with the dreams and your father drew pictures for me to look at before sleeping."

"Did it help?" Aislinn asked.

Levi smiled. "A little."

"Lullabies and blankets and pictures helped cure your nightmares?" Aislinn looked at him incredulously.

"No," Levi admitted. "The things they gave me didn't cure my nightmares but knowing that my family cared so much helped. They knew the things they gave me couldn't fix what was wrong but knowing I was loved wouldn't hurt. So when Paisley made me a blanket, and Talia sang me a lullaby, or Kane gave me a picture I accepted it."

"Did your nightmares go away?"

"Mostly. Now and then I'll have a bad night and I'll play one of Talia's songs or curl up with my blanket and it'll help."

"Was there anything else that helped?" Aislinn asked.

"Grandma and Grandpa sat me down and promised to listen to anything I had to say. I told them that the nightmares wouldn't stop and every time I closed my eyes I saw the things in my dreams. Eventually, I managed to remind myself that the things I saw in my dreams weren't real and that I was safe. Over time the dreams happened less and less. Now the only times I have night terrors is when I'm really stressed."

"What if the things I saw were real?" Aislinn whispered.

"Then I'd tell you talking about it helps and sometimes bad things happen. If you need to talk I'll be here. You don't have to go through this alone." Levi promised.

"What if I don't want to talk about it?"

"Then you don't have to."

"I thought you said talking about it made your night terrors go away," Aislinn said, brows furrowing in suspicion.

"Talking about it helped me but only when I was ready. If you're not ready to talk you don't have to."

"What if I'm never ready?"

"Then you never talk about it. I'll just sit with you for a while." Levi said. They sat in silence while Aislinn thought about what he said and tried to pull herself together. When she felt okay enough to lift her head and look at him without getting upset he smiled at her.

"Do you think you'll be okay for now?" Levi asked.

"Yeah. I'm gonna look for Alex and Thackery." Aislinn said before bounding off.

17.
Thackery

"Whatcha up to?" Aislinn asked.

Thackery jumped. "You scared me." He accused pointing his finger at her.

"I'm not the one hiding in a thicket."

"I wasn't hiding."

"Then what were you doing?"

"Making sure Aunt Paisley can't find me and hug me into submission."

"That sounds like hiding."

"It's not." Thackery insisted.

"Do you want to play?"

"That depends. Will I have to leave this spot?"

"Not if you don't want to."

"Then sure. Hey, what were you doing over here anyway? This isn't your usual spot?" Thackery asked making room for her in the bushes.

"I'm hiding from everyone other than you and Alex."

"Why?"

"I don't want to talk about last night. Alex won't ask because he already knows and you've never been the sort to pry."

"Fair enough."

"Why is Paisley trying to hug you into submission?"

"I accidentally told her that someone said I was useless."

"Does she know you're talking about Haley?" Aislinn asked.

"No. She was trying to hug me until I coughed up a name."

"How did you escape?"

"She decided she wasn't going to get anything out of me with her cruel and unusual torture so she let me go and I decided to make a run for it before she changed her mind."

"Sensible."

"I thought so. Eventually running hurt so I saw this thicket and decided it would make a good hiding spot. After a while, you showed up."

18.
Alex

Alex looked around the room wondering where his erstwhile sibling was when Haley spotted him.

"There you are. I've been looking all over for you. You promised us an explanation." Haley said looming over him.

"I went into the Shadow Realms to find Aislinn. With what's been happening lately I didn't want to leave anything to chance. It's a good thing too. Things were bad when I got there." Alex said with a shudder.

"What happened?" Demetrius asked.

Alex jumped. He hadn't seen him walk into the room. "I found Aislinn trapped in a void. She looked so lifeless and she couldn't Travel home. It was terrifying. I called in the Observers and when that didn't work I asked a Shapeshifter friend of mine to help. Merrick helped me bring Aislinn back earlier this week so I figured my mentor wouldn't mind helping again."

"I don't remember you mentioning a Shapeshifter mentor." Haley accused.

"I could've sworn I told you guys about that earlier. Merrick arrived and discovered one of the Observers was blocking Aislinn's ability to Travel."

"What?!" Haley and Demetrius exclaimed in unison.

"Yeah, it shocked me too. It turns out some of the Observers think Aislinn is the Chosen One destined to save the planet Theopolis."

"Why would they think that?" Demetrius asked.

"Apparently she's the first person to find out about the prophecy and what happened to Theopolis in ages."

"That's stupid. She's just a kid. How's she supposed to save a planet?" Haley questioned.

"I know. Once I explained that I'd also witnessed the prophecy and knew everything Aislinn knew they stared at me insisting that there's no way I could have gotten that information without them knowing."

"How did you get the information?" Haley asked.

"I snuck into the Observer's Station and watched the footage of Aislinn's discovery."

"That's risky," Haley admitted.

"I know but I needed to know how much help Aislinn needed. It's not like I'm planning to break in again."

"Fair enough," Haley replied.

"Merrick threatened to string up the Observer who trapped Aislinn in the Void on charges and Geth tried to force Merrick to train Aislinn as a Chosen One." Alex looked down, shuffling his feet. "I threatened to tell all of my family members that they were going to sacrifice Aislinn and convince all of you not to Travel again."

"I understand. You were mad and while you don't have the right to force us not to Travel if they're going to hurt our family we probably wouldn't be willing to help them." Demetrius said patting Alex on the shoulder.

"Thanks for helping. I appreciate it." Alex admitted.

"It's no big deal," Demetrius said, trying to shrug off the thanks.

"No, it's huge. It might not have been a big deal to you but I was trying to fix this on my own and I couldn't. You showed up and took care of things for me. I never would've had the courage to stand up to those Observers if I didn't know you were backing me up. I was scared but I remembered that you told me courage isn't the absence of fear but choosing to continue despite your fear."

"I don't remember telling you that," Demetrius said.

"You did. It was right after I woke up from a nightmare during my first camping trip. I must've been about seven. Everyone told scary stories before bed. I had a nightmare, freaked out, and woke you up. It would've been easy to ignore me and go back to sleep but you sat up and asked me to speak a little slower. Then you told me to move my sleeping bag over by yours and promised that if anything happened you'd get my dad and he'd fix it. You told me our dirty socks would scare off any ghosts. I wanted to be just like you." Alex admitted.

Demetrius stared at him. "You were scared. It didn't seem right to make fun of you for being scared. Everyone's scared of something and anyone who says they aren't is lying. Besides, it's not like moving your sleeping bag next to mine, and promising to talk to your dad was hard."

"The fact that you didn't think it was a big deal is why I remember it so clearly. You were kind to me because you thought it was the right thing to do. I knew if Aislinn came to me scared I'd help her the way you helped me. Because it's the right thing to do and kindness costs me nothing. You taught me about courage and generosity and that was worth one night of interrupted sleep." Alex explained.

That night the kids brushed their teeth, changed into jammies, and headed toward the living room. The adults grabbed pillows and blankets and started arranging them in a rough circle.

Once the adults had left the children sat up and looked at Demetrius. "Alright, we're going to split into groups. Zinnia, your job is to distract the adults if they come back while we're still Traveling. Haley will wake us up while you're keeping the adults occupied. Alex, Aislinn, and I will try to meet up with Merrick. If we're not back by morning see if you can find backup." With those words, they split up and began to prepare for their mission.

Alex Traveled first since he was the most familiar with Merrick. Merrick floated towards Alex "I've been waiting for you." Merrick had chosen the form of a fluffy green cloud. Merrick frequently appeared in green hues.

"Aislinn should be here shortly with my cousin Demetrius. After what happened with Geth, Dee doesn't want us Traveling alone." Alex explained.

"Your cousin wishes to ensure your safety. Don't worry Geth must get through me to reach you or Aislinn. More importantly, the words you spoke will haunt The Council. It has been ages since a youngling has questioned them. That you did so in defense of your sibling makes it impossible to ignore. They know you have a right to be angry with them for this injustice and it will trouble them." Merrick said, slipping into lecture mode.

Alex looked forward to having Merrick as a teacher. Aislinn arrived next looking around at the rather unassuming surroundings. Merrick had chosen a color-swapped world. The sky was white and a dark orb hung in it. The grass was red in the moonlight. The simple surroundings while alien weren't hard to adjust to. They always looked around to see where they were. The more alien the surroundings the greater the odds that the culture would be hard to comprehend.

"Aislinn so good to see you again. I trust you have recovered from last night's debacle." Merrick said.

"I feel a little better but I think it'll take time. I'm still not certain what they thought I'd be able to do to help. I don't know how to save a planet." Aislinn said before bursting into tears.

Alex walked over to Aislinn. "It'll be fine. Merrick promised to tutor us and already scared off Geth and chided Nithkin. You wouldn't want Dee to show up thinking Merrick made you cry. If Dee and Merrick end up fighting we won't have any protection against Geth or the rest of the Council. So you need to calm down before we wind up in a fight we can't win." Alex argued.

"You're silly. Demetrius wouldn't do that. Haley might but Dee wouldn't. Besides you'd explain things and then it'd be fine." Aislinn said, smiling up at him.

"I'm glad you have such faith in me. Do you think you'll be okay?" Alex asked.

"I'll be fine. After all, I wouldn't want to cause an interplanetary incident." Aislinn said.

"That's good. Soon I shall properly indoctrinate you into the Realm of pomposity and excessively complex shenanigans." Alex declared, puffing his chest out with pride.

"Isn't the word you're searching for induct?" Merrick asked.

"No. I'm certain I meant indoctrinate. After all, it requires a bit of convincing to get children to agree to excessive rules and pomposity. I wouldn't want them thinking the club is something they want to join." Alex insisted.

Demetrius arrived and stared at the green cloud. "You must be Demetrius. Alex told me you were coming." Merrick said.

"That's right. I thought it'd be better to keep an eye on my cousins.

122

They seem to have gotten into a lot of trouble lately." Demetrius explained gifting Merrick with a tight smile.

"Is there anything I can do to put your mind at ease?" Merrick asked.

"I don't know. I thought you'd be mad at me for questioning your motives." Demetrius said looking down in confusion.

"I'm not known for doing what's expected of me. If you tell me not to mix two things because they tend to explode that's fine. If you tell me not to mix two things because we don't do so, we have a problem. Besides, I'm quite fond of Alex. I haven't taken an apprentice in ages and now I've got two of them." Merrick laughed.

"What exactly are Alex and Aislinn going to do as your apprentices?" Demetrius asked.

"I'm going to teach them what I know about Traveling. Afterward, I'll think of something." Merrick insisted.

Demetrius walked over to Alex and Aislinn. "Is Merrick always like that?"

"Merrick likes throwing people off balance. Says it gives greater insight when people are confused. They can't hide as much and truth flows out." Alex added. "One of the first times I met Merrick I got asked what my favorite planet was. I couldn't think of one. Eventually, I just said I loved all of the ones I've seen but there's something about home which calls to me. Merrick said it was a brilliant answer. I asked why Merrick asked me that first instead of my name. Merrick smiled and said my question revealed as much about me as my answer. A name can change but someone's gut reaction tells you all you need to know about them. Merrick said I was a smart child not because I knew so much but because I knew I wasn't done learning." Alex said, smiling at the memory.

"Wow. I think maybe I got off easy. How old were you when Merrick asked you that?" Demetrius asked.

"Seven."

"I definitely got off easy. Do you think Merrick will ask me ridiculously hard questions designed to test my character and strength of will?"

"No. You aren't going to become one of my apprentices. I've got my hands full with these two. Besides, you're older. You've already developed a great deal of your personality. I wouldn't have as much room to instruct. You don't need someone asking you deceptively simple questions to test your mettle. What you need is to ask yourself those kinds of questions. You must ask yourself what kind of person you are and what kind of person you would like to be. Only when you know those answers will any other questions matter." Merrick said and turned away.

"Aren't those the kinds of questions where the answers always change?" Demetrius asked with a trace of confusion.

"They are. Besides, no one can decide the answers to those questions besides you. Perhaps in time, you'll have other questions you need to answer. For now, those two should suffice." Merrick smiled. "Younglings these days. So busy looking for answers they don't stop to wonder if they're asking the right questions. You'll be a fine adult when the time comes. Who knows you might even still be Traveling when that happens."

"You enjoy confusing people don't you?" Demetrius asked, shaking his head.

"Yes. I'm good at it and I like doing things I'm good at. Most people do, I think." Merrick mused.

"Well. You're not wrong. I should head home. I need to explain to the rest of the cousins that you're handling things on this end and we can quit worrying about Aislinn's safety. Since you're not going to hand over your apprentice to Geth and the rest of those cowards." Demetrius explained.

"I'm certainly not and you're right their insistence on putting the fate of Theopolis on a child's shoulders does make them cowards. I'll handle them. You just worry about handling yourself." Merrick said before watching Demetrius disappear.

19.
Merrick

"Your cousin is quite a character. Does Demetrius always act like that?" Merrick asked.

"No. Dee's usually more laid back. Dee's sort of been the de facto leader of the kids in my family. I think Dee resents it sometimes. Being a leader's hard. I find it difficult enough just looking after Aislinn. I can't imagine how hard it would be to feel responsible for all my cousins." Alex admitted. "It's part of why I admire Dee so much. I know I can count on them no matter what."

"I'm glad Demetrius is a good leader and it sounds like your cousin is an even better friend. You're lucky to have someone like that. Not everybody does." Merrick said hoping Alex didn't catch the last sentence.

"Dee's nice and seems to enjoy playing with us and answering all our questions; even the stupid ones," Aislinn explained.

"I see you've joined the mutual admiration society. Still, I had hoped to learn more about my newest apprentices than whether or not the two of you think fondly of your cousin Demetrius. Who I might add I knew nothing about before today." Merrick said, hoping to begin learning more about Aislinn.

"Alex I'll begin testing you tomorrow night. I need to see what your current level is before deciding what to teach you. Aislinn same thing. Don't worry if you end up with different scores. I merely need to know how much I have to teach each of you. If your scores are the same I'll teach you the same things at the same time. If they aren't I'll give you separate lessons while I try to bring you up to the same level. Either way, we should get along just fine." Merrick said, trying to start things off on the right foot. "Any questions?"

"What are you going to teach us?" Aislinn asked.

"Everything I know about being a Traveler and anything else I deem useful. First up, will be teaching you about shapeshifters and how to interact with them. This will help you learn about me so we can work together. Afterward, I'll calculate your scores and design lesson plans. I've told Alex a bit about shapeshifters before but it never hurts to review and this will be new information for you." Merrick explained.

"What if I don't do well on the test?" Aislinn asked with a frown.

"The test is to see how much you already know. There aren't any wrong answers. If you're not sure then either leave it blank or guess and add a question mark next to whatever you weren't certain of. It'll start with simple questions like what is a Traveler and delve into more complicated questions as the test progresses." Merrick explained trying to put Aislinn's fears to rest.

"Will there be word problems? I don't like word problems. I don't care how fast the train is going." Aislinn whined.

"There won't be any questions about trains. I promise. These tests just tell me what you know, how you learn, and a little bit about who you are. How good you are at solving word problems won't tell me any of that." Merrick said with a smile.

"Okay. That's fine."

"We should probably head home. Come on Aislinn, we'll be back here tomorrow night. Besides, Merrick still needs to create the tests and I doubt that will happen if we keep chatting." Alex teased.

"Alright. Bye Merrick. It was nice meeting you and I look forward to seeing you later." Aislinn said waving goodbye to her new cloud-shaped friend.

"Bye Alex. Bye Aislinn. Safe Travels." Merrick said, waving to the siblings as they disappeared.

20.
Alex

The kids woke up and rushed outside after breakfast. Once they'd all gathered Demetrius motioned for everyone to take a seat on the grass. "I met with Merrick. I think they can be trusted. I didn't see any sign of Geth or the others who've been causing problems but that doesn't mean this is over. We need a solution." Dee insisted.

"I thought we solved this already. Merrick tutors Alex and Aislinn and we don't have to worry anymore." Thackery said shooting his cousins a concerned look.

"Aislinn's dreams aren't going to stop. She can't keep remembering what happened to Theopolis and there's nothing we can do to make those images go away. Apprenticing under Merrick only keeps Geth and the others from forcing Aislinn to fix things for them. It doesn't do anything else." Alex said, reaching for Aislinn as she burst into tears.

"Then what are we supposed to do?" Thackery asked.

"I'm not sure. I worry that even with Merrick's help they will try to force her to fix this." Alex declared as Aislinn cried on his shoulder.

"There are rules in place to protect younglings and Travelers. If they break them they'll have to face the consequences." Thackery said, trying to sound convincing.

"True but when the people enforcing the rules are the ones breaking them there's not much you can do. Besides who's going to believe us? If we run around saying there's some kind of conspiracy involving the Council and the Observers all they have to do is deny it." Demetrius admitted.

"Just cause it's hard doesn't mean it's impossible. We'll figure something out. Besides; have we ever failed at something when all of us worked together?" Thackery asked.

"No. We haven't and we're not about to start now. For now, we'll go back to our normal routine. I don't think they can watch us when we aren't Traveling. Pay attention to anything you find while Traveling. If you learn anything important let us know. Alex and Aislinn can ask Merrick for advice about what to do. We're not giving up and we won't give in. Worst case scenario we institute a strike and refuse to Travel until our cousins are safe." Demetrius declared.

Everyone nodded. "Thanks, guys," Alex said with a smile.

"The adults need something fun to take their minds off things and I'd like to see if I can get Aunt Rosemary to smile. She looks so sad." Dee added.

"Send Zinnia to Aunt Rosemary. She loves spending time with

Zinnia," Thackery suggested. Everyone stared at him. "Just because I don't spend a lot of time with Aunt Rosemary doesn't mean I don't pay attention to her. Zinnia's her angel. I asked my mom about it once and she told me if spending time with Zinnia made Aunt Rosemary happy then she'd make sure to let them have plenty of time together."

"I thought you didn't like my mom," Haley said, giving Thackery a dirty look.

"I don't dislike her. I make her sad. She used to call me by the wrong name and then burst into tears. I remind her of someone and it upsets her so I stay away." Thackery explained.

"That's not true." Haley insisted.

"Yes. It is. Just because you hate me doesn't mean I'm a liar." Thackery retorted.

"Guys. This isn't the time." Demetrius interrupted.

"It's never going to be time." Thackery stood up. "Don't pretend you care. We both know that's a lie." Thackery said, wiping tears away before running off.

Everyone stared at the space where he'd been; shocked at what just happened.

"I'm sorry about that. I don't know what got into him." Demetrius said, running his fingers through his hair.

"Of course, you don't." Aislinn retorted.

"What do you mean by that?"

"You haven't been paying attention. I'm shocked by what he

revealed about Aunt Rosemary but the rest of it's been a long time coming. He's your brother and you didn't defend him. Why wouldn't he think you hate him?" Aislinn asked.

Alex turned to Dee unable to hold his tongue. "She's right. Haley accused him of lying and you only intervened when Thackery responded. Either you think Haley's right and your brother would lie about something like this or you don't know Ree well enough to know whether he's telling the truth. Either way, it doesn't sound like you've been a good brother to him."

"Have I really been a bad brother?" Demetrius asked.

Surprisingly Zinnia answered. "Ree said you told him to look after me. He always has time for me. He doesn't care if we play tea party or princess. He's my bestest friend. I asked him if you wanted to play too and he said yous was really busy. Yous a meany head."

"I don't think you understand what's going on Zinnia," Haley interjected.

"I knows you're the one who told Ree he was who-whothless...no good." Zinnia retorted.

Everyone was stunned for a moment. "Wow, Haley. I knew you were a jerk but that's low...even for you." Aislinn responded.

"Did you tell Thackery that he was worthless?" Demetrius asked softly, eyes glittering with unnamed emotion.

Haley didn't say anything, just looked down unable to meet Dee's eyes.

"I have half a mind to tell your parents," Dee admitted, voice cold.

"But my mom…" Haley pleaded.

"Is the only reason I'm considering keeping quiet but you will fix this or I will tell them," Dee ordered.

21.
Thackery

Thackery ran, tears obscuring his vision. He didn't care where he was going as long as it was away from Haley and Demetrius. He kept going until he bumped into something and fell over. Thackery looked up only to realize he hadn't run into an object at all. He'd run into his aunt Paisley.

"Where are you going in such a hurry? I thought you wanted me to teach you about painting." Paisley teased.

Thackery kept his head down not wanting her to see his tears. He wouldn't be able to convince her to let it go twice.

"Any particular reason you're staring at the ground?" Paisley asked, tilting his head up with her fingers. She gasped when she saw him crying. "What happened?" Paisley demanded.

"It doesn't matter."

"Yes, it does. It made you cry." Paisley insisted.

"There are more important things to worry about."

"Thackery Octavius Wallace. I don't want to hear you say you aren't important again. I don't know where you got this idea but I'm not going to let it stand. You're my nephew and I love you. I care about your happiness. Now you can either tell me what's got you down or you can come with me to start your painting lessons. Either way, you're not leaving my side until you're feeling better." Paisley demanded.

"If I choose painting will you promise not to ask what happened?"

"No. But I'll give you time to calm down first." Paisley conceded.

"Why does it matter?" Thackery asked.

"Because you're hurting." Paisley said as if it was obvious.

"Other people are hurting too. Why are you trying so hard to help me when Aislinn and Rosemary need help?"

"There's no law saying I can only help one person at a time. Besides; helping you helps them too. Rosemary wouldn't want you to suffer just because she's having a hard time. Aislinn's problems will still be there when I'm done talking with you so why shouldn't I help you?" Paisley asked

"You could be painting or having fun. Why are you wasting your time dealing with me?" Thackery asked through his tears.

"Spending time with you is fun and I'm going to paint with you. But first, we should get you out of this funk. Learning to paint is easier when you don't have tears obscuring your vision." Paisley teased, wiping his tears away.

"That makes sense."

"Trust me. I'm an artist." Paisley said, striking a pose and making Thackery giggle. "That's better. Now we're gonna grab some aprons. We've got work to do."

"Alright." Paisley grabbed Thackery's hand and led him off to the shed she was using as an art studio. It didn't take them long to reach it. Paisley grabbed her apron and handed the spare to Thackery.

"Put this on and we'll start with the basics. Do you know how to draw?" Paisley asked.

"Sort of. I doodle now and then. I'm not good at it but I can draw basic shapes and people usually know what I was trying to draw even when I don't get it the way I want it." Thackery admitted.

"Drawing's easy to pick up if you're willing to work at it. The more you practice the better you'll get. Painting's more complicated. Some of the ingredients are dangerous so you have to be careful when using them. If you leave them lying around and a child or dog eats them they could get sick. So make sure to clean up after yourself and remember to paint in well-ventilated areas." Paisley instructed.

"What's ventilated?"

"Somewhere with good airflow," Paisley explained.

"Oh. Is there anything else I should know before we get started?"

"Painting is a slow process. You have to draw what you want first, then pick the kind of paint you want to use, and start that process. It's harder than it looks. We'll start on the underdrawing. We're going to go back to the rose garden. We'll do a bunch of rough sketches before

136

deciding which one would make the best complete piece." Paisley said, smiling at him.

"But I'm not good at drawing. It won't look right."

"We don't have to jump into working with paints. This is just to get an idea. It doesn't have to be perfect. But I'd like you to leave your first complete painting as is so you can see how you're improving." Paisley suggested.

"How will I know if I'm getting better?"

"When you've been working on it long enough that you realize how you could make the piece better, pull out a new canvas and paint a new version. It'll let you know how much you've improved."

"Does that work?" Thackery asked.

"Yes. Eventually, I stopped recreating my old pieces because I'd improved them enough that redoing them wasn't worth it. Still, I like to compare my older work to my newest pieces whenever I worry that I'm not improving." Paisley admitted.

"I can do that. Do you know what you want me to draw today?" Thackery asked looking up at his aunt.

"Right now. I want you to walk with me to the garden and draw what you think a fairy garden looks like. Don't worry about getting it perfect. Consider this a lesson in creativity. Are the fairies playful or scary? Do they look like tiny humans or not? Do they sleep in roses or under toadstools or somewhere else entirely? To help you keep the sketches from being hampered by perfectionism don't spend more than ten minutes on the same piece." Paisley demanded.

"What if there's something I want to flesh out into a finished piece?" Thackery asked.

"Then show it to me and we'll discuss what to do from there." Paisley said opening the door and walking outside toward what Thackery thought looked like a garden fairies played in.

They reached the garden with its riot of roses and abundance of colors. Thackery was startled when he saw the second easel. "When did those get here?" Thackery asked.

"I set them up earlier today. It's a fantastic place and I wanted to see what it looked like at dawn. The light wasn't right so I decided to try again later, and I figured it'd be nice to have you start painting in the place where I discovered your artistic abilities." Paisley said, smiling at him.

"You mean it. You want to paint here?"

"Of course. Would I have gone to this much trouble if I didn't?" Paisley asked, raising an arm to encompass the setup. "This is a phenomenal place to paint and I never would've thought to make it into a fairy garden. I've painted rose gardens before but they usually end up being landscapes rather than fantasy pieces. Grandma and Grandpa would be thrilled to hear that their rose garden was the first thing you wanted to paint. The only trouble we'll have is that they'll want to have the piece I make."

"You don't have to give me a painting. It'll make more money if you sell it." Thackery said. He was startled when Paisley laughed.

"Silly goose, I promised the piece to you and I don't break promises. You'll get my piece and we'll give them yours. They'll be thrilled to receive the first Thackery Wallace painting." Paisley explained.

"How do you know?" Thackery asked.

"I'll make you a deal. If they don't like your painting I'll pay for a year of art lessons anywhere your parents pick." Paisley offered.

"What if you lose? Won't that be expensive?" Thackery asked, looking at her in confusion.

"Even if I do lose; I can afford it. If buying you lessons is what it takes to fix your self-esteem and encourage your creativity then I'll do it. You can either draw or we can talk about what made you cry but I don't want to hear any more nonsense about how you aren't worth the effort or expense. Got it?" Paisley insisted.

"I'd like to draw."

"Good." Paisley set a timer for ten minutes. "Remember this is supposed to be a quick sketch so if you're not feeling an idea move on. It may help if you start with small sketches." Paisley suggested flipping her sketchbook to a fresh page.

Thackery opened his sketchbook and thought about what he wanted the piece to look like. His fairies were small creatures of all different sizes and shapes. He didn't know how to draw them since they tended to shapeshift into ordinary creatures when they thought someone was watching.

Unsure how to start he spoke up. "How do you draw a shapeshifter?" Thackery asked, causing his aunt to put down her pencil and turn to him in surprise.

"Are your fairies shapeshifters?" She asked.

"Yes. They shift into normal forms so they don't get caught. It's why no one agrees about what fairies look like." Thackery explained.

"I think I have an idea." Paisley flipped to a new page and drew a mouse standing up on the birdbath and looking at its reflection but instead of seeing a mouse reflected they saw a small winged human with an impish grin. She turned the piece to Thackery. "Would that work?" She asked.

"It's not quite how I imagine fairies to look but it gets the point across."

"Good. Now it's been about ten minutes. Do you have anything to show me?" Paisley asked as the timer went off.

"I have some ideas."

"Okay." Paisley reset the timer.

Thackery grabbed the colored pencils and immediately began sketching a two-tailed blue mouse playing amidst the roses while a small green-skinned person slept curled up on a rose. Behind them, roses bloomed and occasionally an odd color indicated the presence of something that didn't belong. Before anything else could be added Thackery heard the timer go off.

He put his pencils down and Paisley came over to look at his work. "I thought you said you just doodled. This doesn't look like the work of someone who knows nothing about art."

"I've been doodling for years. It's not that impressive." Thackery insisted.

"Yes, it is. Just because it's not on my level doesn't mean it isn't good. Are you sure you haven't had art lessons?" Paisley asked.

"I'm sure. My mom said I can do whatever I want when I finish my homework as long as it's quiet so I usually draw."

"You need art lessons. Come with me." Paisley said, grabbing his sketchbook and walking toward the house.

"Where are we going?"

"To see my parents and fix a grand injustice. You're getting art lessons if I have to pay for them myself. There's no way you can let this kind of talent go unnoticed." Paisley insisted.

"I'm not sure that's necessary."

"Yes, it is," Paisley said, walking faster.

They reached the house and walked into the living room to see Grandma and Grandpa along with Thackery's parents and Kane. "Good, you're all here. Did you know Thackery's an artist?" Paisley asked.

"No. Why?" Thackery's dad asked.

"He took me to the rose garden when I asked for a place to paint; said it looks like a fairy garden. I've been there dozens of times and never noticed that. Today when I asked him to sketch what he'd like to paint he drew this." She pulled out Thackery's sketchbook and showed them his rough sketch.

Kane stared at it. "How long did this take him?" He asked, looking at it intently.

"Ten minutes," Paisley replied.

"Has he taken lessons?" Kane asked directing the question at Thackery's parents.

"No," Thackery's dad said.

"It's a great sketch given the time limit but it's much better than I'd expect from someone who's never had lessons. If this is what his talent's like without training he needs lessons. I'll pay for them if necessary. You can't let talent like this be ignored. It would be criminal not to encourage him." Kane insisted.

"Don't worry about it. I already made a bet with Thackery. If I lose I'll pay for a year's worth of lessons with anyone his parents choose." Paisley said.

"Why did you make a bet with him?" Kane asked.

"He didn't feel confident in his work. So I promised him it would be well received and that if I was wrong I'd pay for lessons."

"Why wouldn't he have faith in his work?" Kane asked.

"Probably because someone convinced him he's worthless," Paisley said, dropping the news with all the subtlety of a bomb.

Thackery's parents looked at him shocked. "Why didn't you tell us someone was giving you a hard time?" They asked.

"You wouldn't have believed me. Besides, it doesn't matter." Thackery insisted.

"Why wouldn't we believe you?" They said pulling him into a hug. Thackery started to cry.

"Do you know who told Thackery he was worthless?" Thackery's parents asked, looking over at Paisley.

"I'm not sure. It has to be someone he respects for him to be upset by it. I thought it was Demetrius but Thackery insists that it wasn't. I'm still not sure if he's telling the truth." Paisley admitted.

"If Dee's responsible he's going to regret it." Thackery's dad said voice hard as he held his son.

"Dee didn't do it." Thackery insisted.

"If he didn't then who did?" Thackery's dad asked.

"It doesn't matter," Thackery said, trying to figure out why they cared.

"Yes, it does." Thackery's mom replied.

Grandma and Grandpa decided to take a closer look at the sketch Paisley and Kane thought proved the need for Thackery to take art lessons. They saw a cute fairy curled up in a rose while a two-tailed mouse played. The backdrop of roses was made more beautiful by the bright spots indicating where magical creatures were hiding. "When Thackery progresses to the point where he's ready to paint his fairy garden we want the painting." Grandpa Smith said.

Thackery looked at his grandparents in shock. His grandpa's eyes and hair were grey but his grandma's were brown. "I told you they'd want your first painting. Now since I won the bet you have to promise not to utter any more nonsense about not being an artist." Paisley demanded.

"Okay." Thackery agreed.

"Does that mean we can have your fairy garden painting when you finish it?" Grandma Smith asked. "I want to hang it in the den."

"You can have it," Thackery promised.

"Now are you going to tell me who destroyed your confidence?" Thackery's dad asked.

"It doesn't matter." Thackery insisted.

"When are you going to learn that you matter?" Thackery's dad asked.

Paisley decided to change tactics. "How would you feel if someone treated Zinnia the way you've been treated?"

"What do you mean?" Thackery asked.

"How would you feel if someone told Zinnia she was worthless?" Paisley questioned.

"Zin's five and she's the youngest. Why would anyone hurt her?" Thackery asked, confused.

"You're nine years old Ree and you're family too. Why is it okay to say hurtful things to you if it's not okay to say them to Zinnia?" Paisley asked.

144

"If someone tried that with Zin they'd have to deal with me and Dee." Thackery insisted.

"Good. Then you agree they hurt you. You have two choices. You can either tell us who it was or we can ask everyone if they know who's been bullying you. I know you don't want to cause trouble but you need to accept that the way you've been treated is wrong. If we don't stop them it's going to continue and they're going to do this to other kids." Paisley explained.

Thackery's eyes widened. "I didn't think they'd bother anyone else. I figured as long as it was just me I could handle it."

"Why would you assume that a bully would restrict themselves to only bothering you?" Paisley asked.

"Because I've never seen him treat anyone else the way he treats me," Thackery explained.

"Just because they're nicer to other people doesn't mean their behavior towards you is acceptable. You deserve better." Thackery's mom said, trying to console him.

"Why is it so important to know who said it. They aren't hurting anyone else and you have bigger problems to deal with." Thackery complained, stomping his feet.

"We talked about this yesterday. Just because there are other problems doesn't mean your problems aren't important." Paisley promised.

"You don't understand. Telling is only going to hurt people."

Thackery insisted, tears spilling as he glared at them.

"Why would telling hurt anyone?" Thackery's mom asked.

Paisley's eyes widened. "Ree isn't telling us because we know him."

Thackery's mom spoke. "Is this true Thackery?" Thackery hunched in on himself and his mom gasped. "Thackery Octavian Wallace I'm going to ask you this one time and you better not lie to me. Did your brother do this?"

"It wasn't Dee," Thackery whispered, unwilling to let his brother take the fall for something his cousin did.

"Then who was it?" Thackery's mom asked.

"If I tell, will you promise to let it go?" Thackery asked a trace of hope entering his voice.

"I can't promise that but I will promise to do my best to make sure this is dealt with quickly and quietly. Now, will you tell me who it was?" Thackery's mom asked voice gentle but firm.

"Haley," Thackery whispered and closed his eyes to prepare for the fallout.

"Just because he's your cousin doesn't mean he gets to treat you like that. I'll talk to him and if he doesn't clean up his act I'll talk to his parents." Thackery's dad insisted.

"You can't. Aunt Rosemary will be devastated. Please don't tell her." Thackery pleaded.

"I can't let Haley get away with this. He'll think his actions are okay if he continues to avoid consequences. But if it'll make you feel better I'll try to avoid telling Rosemary." Thackery's dad promised.

"Thank you. I don't want to make her cry more than I already have." Thackery explained.

"You're a good kid. You know that." Paisley said coming up and ruffling his hair. "Now enough of the serious stuff. I had plans to spend the day with you working on artwork and I think Kane might be willing to show you a few things too."

"Our boy's going to be an artist. You'll have to show us some of the stuff you're working on. The fridge could use some new decorations." Thackery's mom said smiling at him.

"What if it's not good?" Thackery asked looking up at her.

"Then you'll have to make more pieces so we can replace them when you improve." Thackery's mom explained. "Besides I want to see what you're working on in the lessons you're getting."

"Are you going to make sure I get art lessons?" Thackery asked bouncing up and down.

"Yes. You will have as many art lessons as you want." Thackery's dad promised.

"Thanks, dad. I'll study hard."

"I know son. Just remember that art is also supposed to be fun. Why don't you get back to drawing with your Aunt Paisley? We can figure out what to do about Haley by ourselves." Thackery's dad teased.

"Okay. I'll go draw. Can I have my sketchbook back? I want to see about making more sketches so I can decide which ones to flesh out and complete. Aunt Paisley said I could turn the best one into a painting but I need a few more sketches before I can decide." Thackery admitted, reaching for the sketchbook that Grandpa Smith handed back to him. Thackery clutched the sketchbook to his chest and walked towards the door.

"Kane. Do you want to go with us or wait here with mom and dad?" Paisley asked.

"I'll go with you guys. I think I'd like to sketch with two of my favorite artists." Kane added smiling at them.

"We're two of the only artists you know." Thackery teased his uncle Kane.

"Doesn't mean you aren't two of my favorite artists," Kane said walking with them toward the rose garden.

They finished the walk in silence, unwilling to disturb the tranquility of the journey. They arrived and Paisley showed Kane the third sketchbook. "Did you know I was going to come by and draw with you?" Kane asked smiling at Paisley.

"No. But I hoped you might. I figured you'd see me sketching at some point and decided to bring an extra sketchpad just in case. Besides, I know you hate leaving when you're inspired, and this way nobody has to share their workspace." Paisley said as she handed Kane her extra supplies.

"Thanks. I'm glad I got a chance to sketch with you. It's the one thing we did together that none of our siblings wanted to do." Kane smiled.

"I know. Whenever you wanted a break from them or they got too crazy you'd leave to go sketch. You told me once that drawing was one of the most versatile art forms. You could do it anywhere and it didn't require a ton of materials. It's a lot easier to sketch than it is to paint or create sculptures." Paisley admitted.

"True. Thanks for leaving me some supplies to work with." Kane said smiling at Paisley.

"No prob. Let me know if you need to borrow some paint." Paisley replied before turning back to her sketchbook and setting a timer for ten minutes.

Thackery grabbed the colored pencils and started sketching a light green-skinned fairy curled up on a dark green leaf. He added branches coming out of the fairy's scalp and down their back like braids. Finally, he added another leaf covering the fairy so it looked like it was sleeping on the leaf. In the background, he included a kitten keeping watch over the sleeping fairy while roses bloomed around them.

The timer shrieked causing all of them to stop moving. "Kane do you have anything to show us?" Paisley asked.

"I was doing a few sketches but nothing caught my eye," Kane admitted showing his rough impressions of flowers and bushes.

"They look good. Besides nothing says you have to do a certain kind of sketch. It's not an assignment." Paisley teased chuckling at her brother's indignant look.

"Hey, I'm older than you, shouldn't you be respectful of your elders?" Kane asked putting on an exaggerated show of hurt.

"So you admit you're old. I guess it's up to me and Thackery to show you how it's done." Paisley suggested. She handed him her sketchbook with a background of flowers and toadstool houses. Her drawing looked more fleshed out than the sketches she'd done earlier.

"It's good but it needs a focal point. Do you know what you want the piece to be centered on?" Kane asked.

Thackery stared at them in shock. If he'd said something like that to Haley he never would've heard the end of it but Kane just took it in stride and complimented Paisley anyway before offering advice. He wanted to hear Paisley's response.

"I'm not sure. I know I'm going to give this painting to Thackery when I finish. Other than that I'm not sure." Paisley admitted.

"Why is this painting going to Thackery?" Kane asked.

"Because he's the reason it's being painted and he asked if he could have one of my paintings so I promised him this one," Paisley said with a shrug.

"In that case, I think I have a solution. Thackery, what do you think this painting needs?" Kane asked.

Thackery's eyes widened. "It's pretty but it doesn't make me feel anything," Thackery said hoping Paisley wouldn't be mad.

"Huh. I didn't realize I was lacking an emotional component. What emotion should it have inspired?" Paisley asked.

"Wonder. Fairy gardens are magical and exciting. It needs magic and whimsy." Thackery explained gesturing toward the garden.

"Paisley's right. You're an artist. I don't know if I could've explained that so well when I was your age." Kane said smiling at his nephew.

"Alright. Why don't you show us what you've got? I want to see if you've got any other ideas of what you're going to paint." Paisley said eyes glinting in anticipation.

Thackery showed them his drawing of a sleeping fairy. "This is good but it'll be hard to get right. You'd have to get the colors perfect for your fairy to be visible despite the camouflage." Kane suggested.

"Since you're giving your painting to Grandma and Grandpa do you know what emotion you'd like to evoke?" Paisley asked.

"I'm not sure what the emotion's called but I want a sense that anything is possible. As if at any moment a fairy could approach and reveal itself." Thackery said trying to explain his vision.

"You want a sense of childlike wonder. As if anyone who views the painting does so with the eyes of a child. That's going to be harder to accomplish than you'd think. Why don't you try to make the painting reflect the everyday magic children believe in? You could do a split-screen effect with half the painting showing what the garden looks like and half showing what it could be like through the eyes of a child." Paisley suggested.

"Paisley, do you remember the sketch you did earlier where you showed me how to draw shapeshifters using reflections to show true forms?" Thackery asked.

"Yes," Paisley replied.

"Why don't you make that the focal point of your piece. It might not be perfect but it captured what you need." Thackery suggested.

"I'll try that while you work on trying to evoke the feelings you want your piece to inspire," Paisley said smiling at Thackery as they went back to the drawing board.

"Huh. It looks like you two are doing just fine. Are you sure I'm needed here?" Kane asked smiling at them.

"Needed; no." Kane's smile dropped. "Wanted yes," Paisley said as Kane smiled and went back to drawing pictures of roses.

Thackery chewed on one of the pencils as he stared at the sketchpad. Why was this so hard for him? He hadn't had any trouble coming up with the first two pictures. Why was the third one so difficult? Was it that hard to draw something while thinking of what emotion you wanted to convey to your viewers? Thackery shook his head. Doubting himself wouldn't help him solve the problem. He needed to dive in and draw something. It didn't have to be good. It was a sketch, not a masterpiece.

Thackery looked at the garden once more before starting to draw a sprite climbing a rosebush. He made the being spindly and purple with petals instead of hair wearing tiny lavender overalls. Stepping back to look at it once more he drew similar creatures climbing other rose bushes. The purple one was leading while a blue one was in second place and an orange sprite was in last place having stopped to smell the roses.

Thackery flipped to a new page. This wasn't what he wanted to draw and it wasn't all that interesting to him either. Perhaps he was going about this wrong. His fairies were shapeshifters. Why was he drawing other people's fairies instead of his own? He shook his head trying to clear out other people's expectations.

He sketched out a larger version of the garden being sure not to add too many details. He was only making the background of the sketch after all. No need to try too terribly hard. Up close he drew a black kitten looking down at a puddle and in the reflection, he drew an armored sprite riding a fierce cat. The flowers in the reflection changed colors and the leaves were black instead of green.

Thackery flipped the pages again. He drew blue leaves and stems with green skies. The flower colors stayed the same but perched on the tip of a rose was a two-tailed mouse in a bright shade of blue. On the ground was an ordinary black mouse staring up at the blue mouse-like creature in awe. A small black kitten put its paw up to touch a small black catlike being with feathers instead of fur. The catlike being was paw to paw with it as if acknowledging that it was an odd world they lived in where both of them would meet.

Once Thackery was satisfied he'd managed to return to his rendition of fairies he started a new piece on a fresh sheet of paper. This time he started with a wavy line down the center of the paper separating left from right. On the right side, he drew an ordinary garden. On the left, he drew a fairy garden. With toadstool houses, catlike beings with feathers, two-tailed mice, and all manner of other extraordinary things. He drew sprites with branches instead of hair, jackalopes each with its own adorably large eyes.

Thackery never noticed Paisley turning off the timer but he did notice when she cleared her throat before he could turn to a new page. "Do you need help with something?" Thackery asked.

"This is good. Do you want to show it to grandma and grandpa or would you like to keep going?" Paisley asked.

"Do you think they'll like it?" Thackery asked looking up at her hopefully.

"Kid. They were willing to accept the painting based on your first sketch. They'll like whatever picture you choose to draw." Paisley promised.

Kane walked over to inspect the newest piece. "Is this what you've been working on the whole time?" He asked looking at the bisected piece.

"No. I drew a few others too." Thackery said flipping the pages back to show off his earlier attempts.

154

Kane's eyes widened as he looked at all of the sketches. "How long have we been out here?" Kane asked Paisley suspiciously.

"Maybe half an hour. One hour tops." Paisley replied. "Why?"

"Because Thackery made three or four pictures in the time it would've taken me to come up with a dozen rough sketches. He works fast. No hesitation. At this rate, Grandma and Grandpa will be hanging his painting above the mantle instead of on the wall in the living room and that's without art lessons. In ten years I might not be able to afford one of his paintings." Kane teased.

Thackery blushed. He couldn't believe it. Kane thought his artwork was going to be worth something in the future. He pinched himself but didn't wake. This was real. He was an artist.

"You don't have any reason to be jealous. You're one of my favorite artists." Thackery said smiling at Kane.

"One of your favorite artists but not your favorite artist. Why not?" Kane asked.

"Because Paisley is my favorite artist. Don't tell my mom I said that. She's my favorite musician but Paisley's my favorite artist." Thackery said smiling at Paisley.

"Any particular reason why?" Kane asked.

"Because Paisley always has time for me." Thackery paused before whispering a final confession. "Paisley's the first person to believe in me. Not the way parents and grandparents have to where you know they'd say it even if you didn't deserve it. She told me I was talented because she honestly believed it."

Paisley grabbed her nephew pulling him into a hug. "You are talented and wonderful and I'm glad to be your favorite artist even if I don't like the reasons for it. Besides Kane agrees with me so that means he should be your second favorite artist. Right?" Paisley asked.

"That seems fair. I can be your second favorite artist." Kane said coming up behind Paisley and wrapping his arms around both of them.

"You two are my favorite artists," Thackery said smiling at them.

"Now that, that's out of the way, why don't we show grandma and grandpa what you've worked on. They can choose their favorite or give you an idea of what they'd like. It'll give you a taste of what it's like to work with or for a client." Kane suggested.

They walked back to the living room carrying their sketchbooks. "Would you like to see what I've been working on?" Thackery asked, twisting his fingers together.

"Of course sweetheart." His Grandma said patting the seat next to her.

Thackery handed over the sketchbook showing her his pictures. "They're not finished but I thought you might like to help decide what I'm going to paint for you," Thackery said blushing as he watched them look at his work.

"We'll love whichever one you choose." His grandma promised.

"Are you sure?" Thackery asked.

"I like all of them. Which one's your favorite?" His grandpa asked.

Thackery thought for a moment. "The one where I showed the fairy garden next to the rose garden. I think it would look cool with a misty veil separating the two halves." Thackery explained.

"Then work on that one. There's no hurry, draw a bunch of things and when you're done we'll take whatever painting you finish first and hang it up in our house." His grandma promised, making him blush.

"I don't want you to get stuck with a piece you hate," Thackery murmured.

"You've got a lot of talent. Paisley will make sure you don't have to turn in a piece you aren't proud of. But if it makes you feel better you can make us another painting later." His grandpa suggested.

Thackery smiled and held out his hand. His grandpa shook his hand solemnly. "Deal," Thackery promised.

"We'd be happy even if you weren't replacing the first piece. We're always excited to support aspiring artists and it's even more exciting when we get to encourage people we love. Did you know you're the first one of our grandkids to tell us what you want to be when you grow up? So not only are you incredibly talented but you've figured out your gift early." His grandma said, pride leaking into her voice.

"If I ask you to help someone would you?" Thackery asked looking at his grandma

"I'd certainly try. I can't promise anything until I know what the problem is. Unfortunately, not all problems have a solution." His grandma said sounding sad.

"Aunt Rosemary needs help. She's been hurting lots and lots." Thackery said trying to explain. "She's been hurting for a long time and I think I know why," Thackery admitted.

His grandparents' eyes widened. "You do? Who told you?" His grandmother asked.

"Nobody told me. I already knew. I've known for years." Thackery said hoping they'd believe him.

"How did you find out?" His grandpa asked gently coaxing the information out.

"Aunt Rosemary used to mess up my name a lot. She'd try to play with me but she'd forget my name and burst into tears. Eventually, it became easier not to spend time with her. I make her sad." Thackery admitted.

"Why do you think you make her sad?" His grandma asked.

"I remind her of Jasper. It's what she used to call me and there's no way to get Jasper out of Thackery. She misses him and when I'm around she thinks about him. I stopped spending time with her because I didn't want to make her cry anymore." Thackery admitted.

"It's not your fault she's sad. Something happened to her a long time ago and it hurt her. What you explained gives information we can use to help her heal. I wish we'd known earlier. We could have helped you both. That's a big burden to place on a kid." His grandma said hugging him.

"I'm sorry I didn't tell you earlier," Thackery said looking down at his shoes.

"We're not mad at you we just wish you'd had someone to talk to earlier. Is there anything else you think we should know?" His grandpa asked.

"I'm pretty sure you know everything I know," Thackery promised.

"You've kept a lot of secrets. Next time there's a problem you can't solve will you come to one of us instead of shouldering the burden alone?" His grandpa asked giving him a stern look.

"I promise."

"Good. Now go to your parents. They look like they could use a good hug." His grandma said gently pushing him in their direction.

"I love you," Thackery said hugging his parents.

"We love you too sweetheart. Paisley said you've been such a good buddy she'd like permission to continue drawing with you when she visits. You'll have art lessons with an official instructor but she'll give you the occasional lesson or art challenge. What do you say?" Thackery's mom asked.

"I'd love to. Will I have homework?" Thackery asked all but bouncing in his seat.

"If you'd like. If not it can be like it was today. A chance to create or talk about anything that's on your mind." Paisley added.

"Yay!" Thackery yelled jumping up and hugging Paisley. "Thank you, thank you, thank you!"

"I don't think I've ever seen a kid so excited about homework before." Thackery's dad teased.

"I never thought I'd see the day when Paisley agreed to teach someone," Kane added giving his sister a sidelong glance. "This wouldn't by any chance be an attempt to keep me from tutoring Thackery would it?" He asked.

"Of course not. Ree likes me better. I don't have to try. You're just jealous that Thackery's a natural and you had to work to hone your talents." Paisley retorted.

"True," Kane admitted.

Thackery giggled. Who could've guessed that he'd be laughing after the earlier conversations? If this was how his day was going he didn't want it to end. Unfortunately, he knew he couldn't hide out here forever. Soon he'd have to face Demetrius and Haley. He wasn't looking forward to their responses to what he'd said earlier. He didn't know if anyone would want to talk to him after what he'd said to Dee.

22.
Alex

Alex turned to Aislinn once the others had left. "Did Haley ever say anything like that to you?" Alex asked hesitantly.

"He did say I was an annoying brat who needed to learn when to get lost," Aislinn admitted.

"He's going to regret that," Alex muttered, clenching his fists.

"Starting a fight with Haley won't help. He'll just convince himself you're being unfair and add you to the list of people he doesn't trust. If you're going to be mad at him for something, do it because he made Thackery feel bad about himself and prevented Ree from telling Dee what happened." Aislinn insisted.

Alex growled. "What do you mean he prevented Thackery from telling Demetrius what was going on?" Alex asked.

"Do you really think Haley left Demetrius alone with Thackery long enough to tell him anything? I'll bet you anything Haley claimed Ree was causing problems so that if Ree ever tried to complain Dee wouldn't believe him." Aislinn said.

"No wonder Ree ran off when Dee scolded him. Thackery figured

Dee either believed he was a horrible person or didn't think what Haley was doing was wrong." Alex grumbled.

"It's worse than that. If your brother doesn't believe you why would you think anyone else would?" Aislinn asked.

Alex fumed. "Haley's acting like a piece of..."

Aislinn interrupted before he could finish the sentence. "Haley's being awful but you'll get in trouble if you punch him or call him names." Aislinn insisted.

"Fine, but I refuse to let him get away with this. If this isn't fixed by the time you're better I'll tell Uncle Levi myself and to hell with the consequences." Alex insisted.

"We'll tell Thackery we're on his side when we see him. Besides, after the way Zinnia blew up we might not get a chance to nark out Haley. Dee knows what Haley's done so there's no one on Haley's side anymore. At this rate, it won't matter who tells the adults because this'll end before summer does." Alex said with a sigh.

"This is going to be a summer to remember. Who would've thought Zinnia would give Haley and Dee a public dressing down?" Aislinn asked.

"I know what you mean. Having Zin lash out was the thing that made it sink in. I wish Thackery had stayed long enough to hear Zin defending him. Knowing his sister appreciates what he does for her would've meant the world to him." Alex said looking at his sister. "You know I love you, right?" Alex asked.

"I know. You're a great brother and I'm glad you're more involved in my life than Dee is in Ree's even if you frustrate me sometimes." Aislinn admitted.

"I'm glad too. It shouldn't take horrible things happening for siblings to admit they care about each other. I think Dee should've been taking better care of his siblings but it looks like that's going to get fixed too. Zinnia isn't going to let things go back to the way they were before." Alex said.

"True. Nobody's going to forget the conversations that happened today. Too many things were revealed and too many hurts were exposed to pretend nothing happened. The real challenge is going to be figuring out who's going to tell the adults what happened." Aislinn said.

"Maybe Thackery will tell them?" Alex mused.

"Unlikely, but possible. Especially if he runs into one of them before he stops crying. They might not have noticed before but none of them will ignore a crying child." Aislinn admitted.

"Time will tell. Besides, there's a lot more at stake than whether we can avoid telling the adults about Haley." Alex said.

"Do you think you'll be able to get Demetrius to admit he was wrong?" Aislinn asked.

"Won't know until I try," Alex said with a shrug.

"Fair enough," Aislinn replied. "Do you think Dee will try to fix things with Ree?"

"That depends on whether or not Dee thinks their relationship needs repairing. As long as he thinks things are fine he won't try and fix it." Alex explained.

"Is it bad that I think Dee was a bad brother?" Aislinn asked looking up at Alex.

"No. It's not your fault he didn't pay enough attention to Thackery. All you can do is try to support Ree." Alex suggested.

"Thanks. If it helps I'm pretty sure Ree would've told you what was going on if he thought Haley was mistreating me." Aislinn admitted.

"That means Thackery didn't think there was anything wrong with him being treated poorly," Alex said with disgust.

"We know what's going on so Haley won't get away with it anymore. Worrying about it won't make anything better. When we see Ree we can try to fix his self-esteem." Aislinn suggested.

"Fine, but I hate knowing something's wrong and being unable to fix it," Alex complained.

"I hate it too but right now there's nothing we can do. If we barge in and tell the adults without thinking things through it'll make things worse." Aislinn said.

"I hate it when you make sense. It makes it so hard to argue with you." Alex complained.

"It's not my fault I'm better at strategy than you are." Aislinn retorted, sticking out her tongue.

"You are such a brat," Alex said before laughing. "You look silly."

"I may look silly right now but at least I don't have to stay silly looking." Aislinn teased laughing as Alex started pouting.

23.
Aislinn

The cousins prepared for bed and gathered in the living room to nest. Aislinn looked at Alex and wondered if she'd wind up stuck in another nightmare. She shook her head trying to clear the thought..

Everything except the night light went off and the adults left. No one was near Haley and Thackery was between Zinnia and her since he hadn't forgiven Demetrius.

Aislinn sighed. Who would've thought there'd be so much drama. When she arrived she assumed having to explain to the adults that her dreams terrified her would be the worst of it. Days later brothers were turning on each other, conspiracies were being revealed and family secrets had come to light. She'd been told she was the prophecy child, become an apprentice to an alien Traveler named Merrick, and discovered she might know the real chosen one.

Aislinn wondered how she was going to fix things. If she was the prophecy child she needed to be trained, something the Observers seemed strangely unhappy about.

Aislinn tried to think of other things but the longer she lay there the more she was certain the Observers considered her expendable. They didn't care if she was the prophecy child or not. If she saves Theopolis the Observers would try to take credit. If she fails, she'll be blamed.

Her thoughts spiraled darker and darker as the night wore on. She wanted to Travel. If she was Traveling she might be able to think about something other than what the Observers had planned for her. If the a planet didn't hang in the balance she'd be tempted to tell the Observers to solve it themselves.

Aislinn wondered why she felt so responsible for the inhabitants of a planet she knew nothing about a week before. She woke frequently; hearing the screams of Theons as their planet mutated during a level six extinction event. Her desire to save them was affecting her daily life. She couldn't stop thinking about what they'd gone through.

Aislinn looked over at her brother wondering what he'd do if he knew the path her thoughts were taking. Even after returning home she hadn't escaped the nightmare. The problem with being afraid of things that happened is that you know it's real. She would never be the same. Never. The word echoed through her mind like a funeral bell.

Things were different now. She'd suffered as she witnessed the xenocide which occurred on Theopolis. Even after witnessing it she still couldn't believe it had happened. She felt detached from the horror of it all as if letting herself feel would result in the kind of breakdown she'd never recover from. Whenever she closed her eyes she saw the sticky blue fog rolling in killing and mutating everything in its path.

How could something that looked like candy do so much damage Aislinn wondered thinking about the syrupy consistency of the blue miasma that replaced the atmosphere on Theopolis. If you didn't know how dangerous it was you'd think it was pretty. She shuddered. Having seen what it did to the Theons she doubted she'd ever be able to eat blue candy again.

Why wasn't she getting better? Even knowing there was a plan in place to try and save Theopolis wasn't enough to comfort her. She still woke screaming in the night. Perhaps she always would. The thought saddened her but she knew it was likely. She wasn't equipped to handle the things she'd seen. She didn't know if anyone was. Under the circumstances, she thought she was holding up quite well. Not that anyone seemed to acknowledge that.

She could've gone catatonic unwilling or unable to accept what she'd seen. Instead, she'd promised to do everything in her power to ensure that someday Theopolis would be inhabitable again. She wished she knew how she was going to pull it off. She was still a child. How could she succeed when people older and wiser than she had failed?

Aislinn didn't care if it was a long shot. She'd never be able to live with herself if she didn't at least try. Besides, Merrick had promised she wouldn't have to do it alone.

Aislinn began the ritual to enter the Shadow Realms. It was harder to do than earlier. She shook her head, focusing on a place to think.

She saw a bright blue sphere and focused on it. It grew closer and she set herself down on the lavender ground. She was alone and felt grateful she didn't have to worry about making a good impression. She wished things were different. That she could get the screams out of her head. Could close her eyes without fear of what she'd see or worse....remember.

Aislinn looked at the sky; she couldn't see any stars but the two moons circling the sphere were beautiful. The light they cast allowed her to see the varying shades of blue and purple which made up the planet. She didn't care what she looked like tonight but the usual violet glow surrounded her.

Aislinn wondered why she felt more at home in an alien world than she did on her own. Was she destined to never fit in? What made her so unlikeable? Surely, somebody enjoyed her company.

Somehow she was going to convince people to let her save a planet and return the natives to their homeland. She smiled at the thought of everyone's expression when they found out she solved a problem the adults couldn't. Not that it was hard to outperform adults. They tended to think inside the box and Aislinn preferred to avoid even thinking of a box. She was more of a nonagon girl.

169

As Aislinn was thinking this, she noticed a glowing pink box. The box seemed non-threatening so Aislinn decided to look for a tag. Aislinn looked at the box and was startled to see her name on it.

To Aislinn from Merrick.

p.s. I hope this helps.

p.p.s. tell Alex I left them a box as well. Both boxes contain unique items that cannot be traded or transformed so remember which one's which.

Aislinn blinked, rapidly. The gesture made her want to burst into tears. Aislinn opened the box. Inside was a small brown book and a glowing violet pen. She opened the book to the first page. It was blank. She flipped through the pages but all of them were blank. She lifted the book and peered inside the box wondering if she'd missed something. At the bottom of the box was a note.

This book was intended to serve as a diary and a place to store important information. Place the information in the journal and label it with the pen provided. When done using the journal, tap the pen to the cover and ask the book to lock. This will keep everything secure. To unlock ask the book to unlock. Your book can also connect with my book and Alex's. Ask the book to send a message to your intended recipient or write To: followed by their name and it will send the information when the message is completed. Send me a message if you need more information.

   -Merrick

Aislinn stared at the unassuming journal. Besides, even if the journal was normal the glowing violet pen wasn't. Aislinn wondered if she should write in the journal or wait to see if Alex got something similar.

Everything about the gift seemed harmless but she knew she wouldn't be telling many people about the present. Keeping its existence a secret would allow her the time required to find out if it was safe.

Aislinn shuddered when she remembered why she'd come to this quiet planet in the first place. She'd been hoping to outrun her problems. Unfortunately, it wouldn't work. She wasn't the girl she'd been a week ago. She was scared all the time and it took everything she had not to cry. If she started crying she wouldn't be able to stop so she didn't cry.

The tears wouldn't help anyway. All they'd do is confirm everyone's suspicions that she was too damaged to do anything alone. Worse she didn't know if she'd be allowed back to the Shadow Realms if they thought Traveling posed a danger to her.

If she got banned from the Shadow Realms she couldn't save Theopolis. Aislinn promised herself it wouldn't come to that. She didn't know how she'd prevent that outcome but she would. Besides, what kind of person would she be if she didn't do everything in her power to help the Theons return to their home planet.

Aislinn looked around wondering how long it had been before deciding to return home to sleep. She'd wasted enough time feeling sorry for herself. She could've written something in the journal but she wanted to make sure it was safe first. A week ago she would've been happy to receive an unexpected present. Now she worried about the strings attached and if they could be used to hurt her. With those thoughts swirling in her head she began to travel home.

24.
Alex

"I'm scared. Watching what happened to Theopolis was terrifying. The only thing keeping me from breaking down is a desire to be strong for Aislinn. What do I do when that's not enough to keep the truth from crushing me?" Alex asked looking at Merrick desperate for answers.

"You don't have to be strong forever. Aislinn loves you and wants you to be okay. I'll listen anytime you need and when possible I'll answer your questions." Merrick assured him.

"I'm worried about seeing Theopolis' destruction when I close my eyes. I don't want to be afraid all the time but I can't help it. Knowing something can destroy an entire planet like that without warning is horrifying. The Theons were so scared and helpless. It was awful Merrick. Watching it secondhand nearly destroyed me and Aislinn was watching it as if they were there. How do you recover from something like that?" Alex asked with tears in his eyes.

Merrick paused for a minute. "The truth is you don't. When something that bad happens you reach a point where you can't ever be the way you were before. Time splits into before the event and after the event. From there you find your new normal and try to deal with what that means." Merrick admitted.

"Do you know how I can help Aislinn deal with what she saw?" Alex asked.

"You won't," Merrick said holding up a hand to forestall any interruptions. "We will. As far as I'm concerned helping Aislinn recover from trauma is merely an extension of my mentoring duties."

Alex smiled feeling better than he had when he'd arrived. He wasn't okay. Not by a long shot but this had helped. "Thanks, Merrick. You're the best." Alex added smiling at one of his oldest friends.

"You say that now but I'm not sure you'll feel the same once I've started assigning you homework." Merrick teased.

"I don't care. You're awesome so any homework you give should also be awesome." Alex said with a grin.

"Unfortunately, I don't think you'll agree in a moment. Your first piece of homework is to find an appropriate outlet for the feelings you've been having. It doesn't matter what kind of outlet as long as you don't hurt anyone. I expect you to tell me about it the next time you see me. I suggest talking to someone or keeping a journal." Merrick suggested.

"Who could I talk to that would understand?" Alex asked.

"Me, Aislinn, any of your cousins or a fellow Traveler." Merrick retorted.

Alex sat there in stunned silence for a moment. "Why a journal?" Alex asked.

"Because I made you one. It's a special journal. It's connected to other journals but nothing in it can be read by anyone else unless you tap that section and verbally request it be sent to someone else's journal. So if you wanted me to read a section you'd tap the entire section and say 'send to Merrick'. I'm also sending one to Aislinn. Your journals also contain an extra feature. They can be used to hide information." Merrick smiled when they saw Alex's look of confusion.

"Huh?" Alex asked.

"You can use the journals to compile evidence and clues," Merrick explained.

"Why?" Alex questioned.

"Because Aislinn wants to fix Theopolis and your sibling accidentally uncovered evidence of conspiracies. I thought it would be smarter to allow you to compile data so you can send it to me and let the adults handle it next time. It'll decrease the risk of you two getting hurt." Merrick admitted.

"Won't that put you in danger?" Alex asked.

"I've been working undercover trying to find out who's been causing problems in the Shadow Realms for years. This doesn't change anything for me. It just makes things safer for you two. Besides, you aren't the only informants I have. The journals make sure no one can steal information or use it against us. Even if I do show someone the information they won't be able to tell where it came from." Merrick explained.

"So it's a way to keep us safe and allow us to store all the information in one place?" Alex asked.

"Yes. You don't have to use that function of the journals but if you do it'll be safe. Just promise me you won't go looking for trouble. Watching you and Aislinn suffer was heart-wrenching. Why, you may have scared a century off my lifespan." Merrick said.

"So that's why you've been choosing a different form every time I see you. You're trying to hide your white hairs." Alex teased.

"You'd like to think that, wouldn't you? Alas, you have no way of knowing whether or not I'm serious." Merrick insisted.

"I didn't really scare you enough that you lost a century of your lifespan; did I?" Alex asked sounding worried.

"No. I didn't lose one hundred years of my lifespan because of you but I may have gained some white hairs due to the last few days. I'd prefer it if you and your sibling could stay out of trouble for a little bit. I need to recover from the shock to my system. I've never had apprentices before and within days of taking you two on you uncovered a massive conspiracy. I wasn't expecting that." Merrick admitted.

"Do you want to stop mentoring us?" Alex asked voice tight with fear and emotion he didn't want to name.

"No. I don't regret being your mentor but I would like you and

Aislinn to be more careful in the future. Bad enough you stumble into these kinds of things on accident. I'm certain you'll soon be looking for this kind of trouble. Especially if I'm right about the quest Aislinn has chosen to undertake." Merrick added.

"We don't usually go looking for trouble. Aislinn stumbled into it by accident. Then I had to find out what was scaring my sibling. If we'd known what was going on we'd have asked for help sooner or tried to avoid it entirely.." Alex admitted.

"Well, that's good. Now we just need to convince Aislinn it's okay to ask for help. I'll have to work on gaining their trust." Merrick said.

"You talked Aislinn into returning to their body and they trust me. So if I trust you and Aislinn trusts me then you have some of their trust. The rest will come when they know you better." Alex assured Merrick.

"I know. Aislinn will learn I have their best interests at heart and I'll teach my newest apprentice to come to me when they need help." Merrick insisted.

"Okay. It shouldn't take too long to do." Alex promised.

"I hope you're right. It would be embarrassing if my apprentice didn't trust me and I had to find out what they were up to from someone else. Why the shame of hearing about which arrests they were involved in second-hand would be too much for this poor shapeshifter. I might wind up shapeshifting into a chameleon just so I can hide my face." Merrick whined.

"You're silly." Alex laughed. "Thanks."

"For what?" Merrick asked.

"Distracting me," Alex said smiling at the look of pride on Merrick's face.

"Can't get anything past you can I? Next thing I know you'll be gearing up and taking my job." Merrick teased ruffling Alex's hair.

"I can think of worse things to do with my life," Alex said with a grin.

"I'm sure you could but it'll be a while yet before you get the chance to do this kind of work. I'd prefer if you waited before deciding on a career so fraught with danger." Merrick said in all seriousness.

"I know but that doesn't mean I can't do it in the future," Alex said cheerfully.

"Younglings. They never bother to appreciate the advantages of youth." Merrick sighed. "Besides, the older you get the less likely you are to visit the Shadow Realms. I'd like to enjoy having apprentices for a while."

Alex looked at Merrick in shock. He'd never thought about it before but it was true. Most species seemed to follow an unspoken rule that Traveling was primarily for younglings. He'd never found out why and wasn't sure he would. Something about growing up made it harder to Travel through the Shadow Realms.

Merrick looked sad so Alex tried to think of something to cheer his mentor up. "My cousin Demetrius is fourteen and my oldest cousin Haley is fifteen and both of them still Travel. Dee doesn't Travel as much as they used to but that's because Dee's Traveling is restricted. Dee tried to stay in the Shadow Realms permanently so the Observers limited their ability to Travel. I'm not sure why Dee wanted to stay forever but that's not the point. If my cousins can still Travel and they're teenagers I should be able to Travel for a few more years." Alex insisted.

"I think I know why the Observers put your cousin on restriction but I'm glad you don't plan to cease visiting me anytime soon," Merrick admitted pulling Alex in for a hug that smelled of fur and incense. Alex decided that the scent while unusual wasn't offensive. He hugged Merrick back, grateful to have the being as his mentor.

"Do you think Aislinn and I will be able to gather evidence to help you take down the bad guys?" Alex asked.

"You did break open my case and uncover one of the co-conspirators and Aislinn has uncovered a couple of secret operations before," Merrick explained.

"How did Aislinn do that?" Alex asked confused.

"Mostly by being in the wrong place and witnessing something going down. Aislinn's not known for letting things go." Merrick admitted.

"So you want me to keep an eye on things and include my observations because it will help you protect Aislinn and solve cases,"

Alex said.

"It's also to ensure you don't feel a need to go running headlong into danger. I'm trying to protect you too Alex." Merrick said exasperated.

"I know but I'm used to protecting Aislinn so it doesn't always occur to me to protect myself," Alex said with a shrug.

"You kids are going to make my hair white. Just because your younger sibling needs to be protected doesn't mean you don't as well." Merrick held up an arm to forestall any complaints. "You matter too. I'm going to teach you the value of self-preservation if it takes me a century. Repeat after me. 'I will not rush headlong into danger.'" Merrick insisted glaring at Alex until he agreed.

"I will not rush headlong into danger," Alex grumbled.

"I am worthy of protecting." Merrick coached continuing to glare at Alex.

"I am worthy of protecting." Alex wanted to argue but Merrick's face convinced him not to.

"I will do my best to ensure I survive all dangerous situations." Merrick continued.

"I will do my best to ensure I survive all dangerous situations." Alex paused. "Is this necessary?"

"Yes, now there's one more line. Repeat after me. 'I will ask for help from those I trust rather than endanger myself unnecessarily."

"I will ask for help from those I trust rather than endanger myself unnecessarily," Alex repeated while rolling his eyes.

"Good. I know that wasn't fun for you but it will help me sleep better knowing you're safe and will do your best to remain that way." Merrick admitted breathing a sigh of relief.

"I'm not stupid. I did ask for help when I needed it." Alex insisted.

"Yes. You did ask for help but you didn't do so before seeing the destruction of Theopolis. I wish you hadn't seen that." Merrick said sounding sad.

"Was I supposed to just let Aislinn suffer?" Alex asked getting angry.

"No. Theopolis is a problem that should've been dealt with ages ago. Your defense of your sibling is admirable but I wish it hadn't been necessary. I wasn't trying to anger you. I was trying to explain that I wish you hadn't suffered." Merrick explained.

"Oh." Alex's indignation collapsed like a deflated party balloon. "I'm sorry I yelled at you. It was rude of me." Alex admitted.

"No harm done. Just remember to be careful about the words you choose youngling. Words once spoken can never be unspoken. In time you will learn that I only have your best interests at heart. You once trusted me implicitly. I hope you will learn to do so again." Merrick said sounding hopeful.

"I was very young when we met. I hadn't learned to be wary of strangers. I don't trust you as much because you lied to me. It made it hard not to wonder what else you may have lied about. Ideally, I would've been given time to process my feelings before seeing you again but time is a luxury I didn't have. Aislinn needed help and you were the only Traveler I knew who might respond in time." Alex admitted.

Merrick's eyes closed and the being seemed pained. "I did lie but I didn't intend to hurt you. The only thing I've ever lied to you about is what I did and even then it was a lie of omission. I couldn't tell you I was working undercover for the Observers. They flag all mentions of them and members are forbidden from revealing themselves except under very specific circumstances. I told you as much of the truth as I could. I can't promise I will tell you everything because the investigation is ongoing but I will tell you what I can as soon as possible."

"I wasn't expecting to find out you'd lied to me. I know why now but when I found out I didn't. I just knew you were keeping secrets and were part of a group that let Aislinn get hurt." Alex explained.

"If I'd known what would happen to your family I would've stepped in sooner. My bosses wouldn't have been happy about me blowing my cover but they would've understood. Besides, I'm a shapeshifter. If I needed to create a new cover I could've. It's hard for me to stay in one shape for long periods. It's why I kept showing up in various green forms when you were younger. I needed to shift but keep to a theme so you'd be able to recognize me despite the changes in my appearance." Merrick admitted.

"I can turn my astral form into any guise I want. My physical form is a little more complicated but I'm still mostly limited by my imagination. If I can't picture what I'm trying to shift into it isn't safe to attempt the transformation." Merrick admitted.

"Are there rules about the forms you can take?" Alex asked.

"Yes. The most well-known rule is the one about mass. I can take any form I choose but I have to maintain the same weight. This means that if I want to take the form of a larger creature I need to ensure my bone density is lower or I can't do it." Merrick explained.

"Is it hard to remember the rules?" Alex asked.

"Not really. There are exceptions to most rules. Since I often appear in an astral form I don't have to worry about following any of the normal rules. When I'm in a physical form anything I try that's impossible doesn't work. I either can't attain that form or need to do more research before trying again. I also cheat a lot. I'm fond of opposable thumbs so whenever possible I add opposable thumbs so I can grasp things with ease." Merrick admitted smiling at Alex's gobsmacked expression.

"You can hack any creature or form you want and you usually do it to add opposable thumbs?" Alex asked dumbfounded.

"Yes. What else would I use it for? Shape-shifting is a lot like evolution. If it's not useful it doesn't get kept and if it is useful add it." Merrick explained.

"I know you're a Traveler but I often forget that shapeshifters have their own culture and other times it's so obvious that I don't know how I can forget our differences," Alex admitted.

"Shapeshifters tend to confuse people. Most of the rules get thrown out the window when everything about someone can change." Merrick said before changing the subject.

"Look, there's a lot I need to teach you and not a lot of time. So sit down and prepare to learn things."

"I thought you weren't going to teach me anything until after the placement tests you're going to give me and Aislinn," Alex said wrinkling his brows in confusion.

"Aislinn hasn't broken into the Observers' compound. You have. So I'm going to explain why you shouldn't do it again." Merrick said with a pointed look.

Alex stared at his mentor for a moment wondering how a fuzzy green alien could pull off a look of parental disappointment. He shook his head deciding he probably didn't want to think too hard about why it was so effective. "I wouldn't have done it if it wasn't necessary," Alex whined.

"I'm not arguing about your reasons for doing it the first time. I'm just making sure you won't do it again." Merrick insisted.

"Sometimes Merrick you're a total party-pooper," Alex complained

"They know their place was infiltrated so they're going to beef up security. They won't get caught unaware again. As my apprentice, your behavior reflects on me. So if you're caught sneaking into places and stealing things I'll get busted too." Merrick said.

"What if I don't get caught?" Alex asked with a smirk.

"You'll get caught. I work with them occasionally so even if no one else noticed you sneaking in I would. They've already closed all the openings you used to pull it off the first time and no that isn't meant to be taken as a challenge. You snuck in once to save your sibling and you got away with it under those circumstances. If you do it again they won't be as lenient." Merrick explained.

"You're no fun," Alex whined.

"I don't care. I'm your mentor. It's my job to help you grow up and become a decent being. I'm not supposed to encourage reckless behavior." Merrick snarked.

Alex's eyes closed as he thought about it for a minute. Perhaps he was being a bit harsh. Merrick may have lied to him about a few things but they had been working undercover. Besides, Merrick was right. He'd gotten away with breaking into the Observer's headquarters and stealing one of their outfits. It wouldn't be wise to push his luck by trying again. "What if I need information they have?" Alex asked.

"If I think your reason is justified I'll look for it myself. Do you understand?" Merrick asked rising to an imposing seven feet with arms crossed and a scowl fixed firmly in place.

Alex gulped. "I understand." He said trying not to show how shaken he was.

"Good. You don't want to know what punishments I've got lined up if you decide to break my rules. The rules are in place to keep you safe. The Observers aren't usually aggressive but they hoard knowledge as obsessively as dragons hoard gold." Merrick explained.

"Wait, dragons are real?" Alex asked.

"We're in the Shadow Realms. One of the first things you learn is that if you Travel far enough anything is possible. I've taken the form of a dragon many times." Merrick admitted.

"Any particular reason you chose a dragon?" Alex asked.

"I was bored and flying is awesome," Merrick said with a shrug.

"Will you show me your dragon form sometime?" Alex asked.

"Maybe. You should start studying for your placement exam. When you've proven yourself I'll show you what a dragon looks like." Merrick offered.

"That sounds suspiciously like a bribe but I don't care. Dragons are awesome!" Alex exclaimed grinning from ear to ear.

"It's good to see you have your priorities straight. I'd hate to think you forgot to utilize situational awareness." Merrick said dryly.

"There's no need to be sarcastic." Alex insisted.

"Good. You can prove it when I test you later." Merrick said with a vicious grin.

"Was it really necessary to swap all your teeth out and replace them with swords?" Alex asked.

"How do you know this species didn't have sword teeth to start with?" Merrick asked.

"Because even if they did have sword-like teeth they wouldn't have hilts on them." Alex retorted.

"I stand by my previous statement." Merrick insisted.

"Sure. It's not like you just got done explaining to me that you customize your forms whenever possible. I'm sure there's a species that has sword teeth complete with hilts and handguards." Alex snarked.

"You never know," Merrick replied. Alex raised an eyebrow and gave his mentor a look of disbelief. "Fine. I made that part up." Merrick admitted.

"I'm glad you decided to stop insulting my intelligence by pretending the sword teeth weren't an intentional upgrade designed to frighten me," Alex said smiling as Merrick pouted.

"All my plans ruined. Do you know how hard it's going to be to find something else that will amuse me as much as teasing you?" Merrick asked.

"I don't know nor do I care." Alex retorted.

"Ouch. Younglings these days. No respect for their elders." Merrick groused.

"I'd find it easier to respect you if you didn't insist on being ridiculous and complaining about stupid things," Alex replied.

"Taking you on as an apprentice is looking more troublesome by the minute. I'm not going to be having much fun while I teach you."

Merrick paused before smirking at Alex and pointing. "You're a killjoy. As your mentor, it's my job to annoy you." Merrick insisted.

"Right. This has nothing to do with me not being as easily impressed as I was when I was four." Alex teased.

"Perhaps I should start calling you bratling since you seem so intent on getting me to act less professional," Merrick suggested.

"There's no need to go that far. Sticking to teasing you seems remarkably kind of me. If you're looking for someone to respect you try Aislinn. They don't have any reason to resent you. As long as I insist that my issue with you is personal none of my family will intervene." Alex admitted.

"Alright. You've made your point. I won't object to you working out any lingering animosity by teasing me as long as you promise not to sic your family on me and agree to act respectful in public." Merrick conceded.

"Just for that, I'll cut my initial plans short by two weeks," Alex promised.

Merrick's eyes widened. "What would you have done if I hadn't capitulated?"

"Extended the punishment by six weeks and asked Demetrius for help," Alex said with a vicious grin.

"Suddenly I'm feeling very understanding of your newfound penchant for teasing. I'd feel sorry for your enemies if they hadn't crossed you by breaking the Traveler's Code." Merrick admitted before a vicious grin appeared on the being's face. "You wouldn't mind giving me a list of appropriate punishments for beings who intend to force Aislinn to act as the Chosen One would you?" Merrick asked.

"I'd be delighted to. I'm sure if I explain, my cousins will help me come up with a set of suitable punishments so everyone gets the message that harming our family will always end badly.....for you." Alex promised, his eyes lit with unholy glee.

"I'm going to ignore the demonic glow in your eyes since my suggestion provoked it. I'd hate to have to go back and arrest myself for breaking a law I think is stupid. Just remember to run the punishment by me before pulling it. It'll give me time to make sure it isn't lethal or illegal." Merrick suggested.

"Okay." Alex agreed. It took all the self-control he had to keep himself from rubbing his hands together and cackling like a madman.

"I feel like I should be concerned right now," Merrick admitted.

"I'll try to contain my vindictive glee at the thought of making beings who endanger children suffer," Alex said dryly.

"I appreciate it," Merrick responded.

"Now that the obligatory warnings are out of the way do you have anything else to discuss or can I go home?" Alex asked.

"I believe I promised to give you a refresher on shapeshifter etiquette." Merrick said.

Alex groaned. "I'd hoped you'd forgotten."

"I haven't. Shapeshifters dislike using gendered pronouns because we have an infinite number of genders, and guessing incorrectly is rude. So we stick to gender neutral pronouns and ask others to do the same in our presence. Travelers tend to do the same to avoid offending anyone." Merrick explained.

"That actually makes a lot of sense." Alex said.

"Now we're done. Just remember to let Aislinn know the journal's from me." Merrick reminded.

Alex nodded. "I'm going home now. Thanks for the journal. See you later." Alex said, beginning the ritual to return home where he promptly fell into a deep sleep.

25.
Aislinn

Aislinn woke up. She wanted to talk to Alex about her dream but was startled to realize she was holding something. She looked down to see the journal she'd dreamed about. She'd never had anything come with her from the Shadow Realms. She wondered if any of the Cousins had heard of this.

Aislinn jumped out of bed and looked around for Alex but didn't see him. She decided to get breakfast before continuing her search. She walked into the kitchen to find Haley shoving Thackery. "What's wrong with you?" Aislinn asked as she helped Thackery to his feet.

"He got me grounded," Haley complained.

"I did not." Thackery retorted, brushing himself off.

"You told my parents I bullied you," Haley whined.

"I spent yesterday with Aunt Paisley and Uncle Kane. Paisley thought Demetrius was bullying me and my parents asked if it was his fault. I wasn't going to let Dee take the fall for you. They were sitting with Grandma and Grandpa when this happened. I told them I didn't want Aunt Rosemary to find out and they said they'd try but insisted this couldn't continue." Thackery replied.

"You got me grounded" Haley insisted.

"Didn't you listen to anything Thackery said? They were going to punish Dee if he didn't tell them who it was. If you hadn't bullied him you wouldn't be in trouble. Now leave before I tell Uncle Levi about this." Aislinn threatened.

"No need. I've seen enough. Perhaps I should tell my wife. It would break her heart to find out what her son's been up to but she'd be more upset if I let it continue." Levi's voice was so cold Aislinn shivered at the sound of it.

Haley's eyes widened in fear and confusion. "I didn't think..."

Levi interrupted his son, his voice somehow getting colder. "That's right. You didn't think. You figured if you harassed Thackery he'd tell us he'd lied and things could return to normal. I don't think I've ever been so ashamed to call you my son." Levi said, turning away from Haley. "Go to your room. I don't want to see you until dinner. If I have to step in again you won't like the consequences." Levi promised.

Haley slunk off to his room dragging his heels. Once Haley was out of sight Levi turned to her and Thackery. "I'm sorry you had to see that. Should I see if someone has a first aid kit?" Levi asked Thackery who shook his head. "Alright. Let me know if you need anything." Levi insisted before leaving.

Thackery turned to Aislinn. "That was freaky." He said with a dazed look.

192

"Yeah. Uncle Levi's always been super nice so hearing him like this was strange. It was even weirder when he acted friendly afterward." Aislinn said with a shudder.

"It was pretty jarring," Thackery said, pausing for a bit before continuing. "Do you think Dee will be mad when he finds out Haley got grounded because of me?" Thackery asked.

"No. He laid into Haley after you left, the rest of us laid into him too. Eventually, Haley left and when Dee asked if he was a bad brother Alex said yes. So if you're worried about telling the truth for fear of Dee blaming you; don't be." Aislinn said, trying to reassure him.

"Dee told Haley off?" Thackery asked, startled.

"He didn't want anyone picking on his baby brother," Aislinn promised.

"It's a nice thought but I'm sure if Dee wanted to help me he would've done so years ago," Thackery murmured.

"Ask Alex if you don't believe me. Dee was an idiot for not figuring out what was going on. Zinnia figured it out and she's five. She also laid into Haley for making you feel bad. She called him a meanie-head and told Dee what he said to you. I don't think I've ever seen Dee as angry as he was when he learned that Haley called you worthless. He's not been the best brother in the last few years but it's not because he doesn't care." Aislinn promised.

"If Dee cares about me why didn't he notice what was

193

happening?" Thackery asked.

"I don't know Ree. The only explanation I could think of that makes any sense is that he was so caught up in his problems he didn't notice yours. Maybe it has something to do with the reason he wanted to stay in the Shadow Realms permanently?" Aislinn suggested.

"I guess. Zinnia really called Haley a meanie-head?" Thackery asked, trying and failing to keep a straight face.

"Dee looked like he wasn't sure if he should scold her for insulting Haley or compliment her for sticking up for you. Zinnia left after telling Dee he'd been a bad brother to her and claiming you were her best friend since you actually spend time with her. Dee ended up asking us if he was a bad brother and Alex said he'd never take someone else's side without hearing me out. You may have been dealing with this on your own but you don't have to anymore." Aislinn promised before hugging Thackery.

"What did I do to deserve friends like you?" Thackery asked.

"Nothing. We're family by blood but friends by choice. The only thing you did to make us like you is; be yourself." Aislinn said, looking away so Thackery could wipe the tears from his eyes.

"Thanks," Thackery said once he'd composed himself.

"You're welcome. Do you mind if I ask you a question?" Aislinn asked.

"You can ask. I can't promise I'll answer but you can ask." Thackery replied.

"Have you ever taken anything out of the Shadow Realms?" Aislinn asked.

"What do you mean taken something out of the Shadow Realms?" Thackery asked, wrinkling his brows in confusion.

"I Traveled and when I arrived I noticed a package with my name on it. There was a note attached saying the journal inside was from Merrick. When I woke up this morning I was holding the journal." Aislinn said, showing him the journal.

"Are you sure it isn't something one of the adults left for you?" Thackery asked.

"Why would they put it in my hand while I was sleeping instead of handing it to me while I was awake. Besides what are the odds that I'd dream about a journal and wake up holding one?" Aislinn asked.

"I don't know. If it's the journal from your dream there should be a note from Merrick. For all you know there's an inscription saying it's from your parents and this is a coincidence." Thackery suggested.

"Maybe I am being irrational. After all, it could be nothing." Aislinn said, sighing before opening the journal. A note fell out. She picked it up and read it aloud.

"Dear Aislinn,

It's Merrick. I thought you could use something to keep a record since it seems like you're going to keep uncovering secret conspiracies. This journal is connected to mine and Alex's. Just say the name of the one you want to see the information and the page numbers and the journal will do the rest. Hopefully, I'll hear from you soon. I thought it would make it easier to reach you in case I'm unable to get to Earth.

Sincerely,

Merrick.

P.S. I expect you to start prepping for your upcoming test. I want to see how much you know about the Shadow Realms."

Thackery stared for a moment. "That's...odd. But, if the journal works as promised you now have a secure means of communication. You can record anything you want and nobody can get to the information. You should still exercise caution but Merrick is encouraging you to compile all the information you can get your grubby little hands-on." Thackery said rubbing his hands together in glee.

"My hands are not grubby." Aislinn retorted.

Thackery sighed. "That would be the part you focused on. Didn't you hear anything else I said?" He asked.

"Merrick wants me to investigate and gave me a journal so I could keep secure records. Try not to get caught snooping but uncover all the dirt I find and stick it in the journal." Aislinn repeated smiling at the look on Thackery's face. "How am I supposed to verify that the journal is safe and secure?" Aislinn asked.

"I don't know. Why do you expect me to come up with all the ideas?" Thackery asked.

"It was your idea to start hunting down information like a magpie looking for shinies." Aislinn retorted.

"What happened to my baby cousin who told me she loved me and had my back?" Thackery asked, pretending to be offended.

"I do love you and I do have your back but that doesn't mean I'm going to ignore it when you're being foolish and unreasonable," Aislinn replied, sticking her tongue out.

"I feel so loved," Thackery said, voice drier than the Sahara desert.

"You should. Normally, I'd be spending time with Alex or giggling with Zinnia but today I chose to grace you with my presence. You should be grateful. Others would kill to be in your position." Aislinn teased.

"I think you might be getting heatstroke. There's no other explanation for why you believe yourself to be more important than me. Surely you've heard of the amazing artiste Thackery Octavian Wallace. Why, his paintings make grown men weep. Angels rejoice when he completes a project." Thackery retorted.

Aislinn collapsed in a fit of giggles. "You are too much sometimes. We should hang out more. I'd forgotten how easily we fell into a rhythm together. We used to hang out all the time during the summers. What happened?" Aislinn asked.

"I think I hit a point where I thought girls had cooties and Haley told me only babies wanted to hang out with kids younger than them. You and Alex spent so much time together I started feeling like a third wheel. You two act more like twins than siblings. You have a better sibling relationship than Demetrius and I ever had. I started wishing things were different and eventually when I realized Dee wasn't going to change I started avoiding you and Alex." Thackery admitted.

"I'm not mad at you. I'm mad at Haley" Aislinn said.

"I'll have to fight my own battles sometime," Thackery said.

"No; you don't. That's the best thing about having family and friends. You don't have to fight your battles alone." Aislinn insisted.

"Aren't you being a tad dramatic?" Thackery asked.

"I think it's reasonable. Besides we're only having this argument because you went years without asking for help. If we knew you'd ask for help when you needed it we wouldn't worry about you as much." Aislinn explained.

Thackery shook his head. "I was handling it," Thackery said but

Aislin shook her head in disbelief.

"No, you weren't. You were fading away into a pale imitation of your former self. I knew something was wrong but I wasn't around often enough to find out what. I should've made sure someone was looking out for you but I thought you'd confide in someone. I'm offering help now because I regret not doing so before. I won't make that mistake again." Aislinn swore.

"Thanks. I think." Thackery mumbled.

"I know it's going to take a while to sink in but we're on your side. Even Uncle Levi is stepping in and if he knows, the other adults either know or will know soon." Aislinn said, trying to reassure him.

"How did we end up in this position?" Thackery asked.

"I've uncovered a couple of conspiracies in the Shadow Realms and we've learned what happens in the Shadow Realms affects the real world. I'm not sure how it works but it has implications I'm not ready to think about." Aislinn admitted.

"Yeah. That's definitely the kind of talk I don't want to have right now. It's far too early to be thinking about the implications of anything." Thackery replied.

"Well, at least we're on the same page," Aislinn said smiling at him.

With that thought in mind, they split up to begin their day.

"Alex has to be around here somewhere." She muttered. She grabbed some cereal and decided to worry about it after she ate. When she was done she rinsed her dishes and put them in the dishwasher before resuming the search for Alex.

"Ouch." She looked up. It was Demetrius. "Sorry about running into you but I'm glad I caught you. I'm gonna say something and I want you to hear me out before responding. I'm not sure what caused you to ignore Thackery but you're going to fix it. He loves you but he's spent years thinking you approved of what Haley was doing. You will fix this or I will make you wish you had." Aislinn threatened.

Demetrius took a step back. "Easy, little firecracker. I promise to talk to Ree. If I'd known what was happening I'd have stopped it." Dee insisted.

"I know that you know that, but Ree doesn't know that Haley doesn't know that, and I'm not sure Zinnia does either. I think Zinnia's madder at you than she is at Haley. She called him a meanie-head but she called you a bad brother in front of us. Zinnia doesn't usually say anything bad about anyone. When Alex broke her doll last summer she cried for a few minutes and didn't talk to him for half an hour." Aislinn said before being interrupted by Demetrius.

"What do dolls have to do with this?" Demetrius asked.

"You didn't break her doll, you broke her brother. Brothers aren't as easy to fix or replace." Aislinn explained.

Demetrius looked like he'd been stabbed. "I didn't mean to break Ree." He admitted.

"Doesn't mean it didn't happen. Now that you understand what's wrong you can work on fixing it." Aislinn said.

"I knew what Haley had done was awful but I didn't think I'd been behaving terribly too." Demetrius paused. "I'm willing to take whatever punishment you deem necessary."

"This was your punishment. I wanted you to understand why I was mad at you and what you'd done. As long as you acknowledge what you've done and work to fix it we're good but if you do anything like this again I will do far worse." Aislinn threatened.

"Sometimes you scare me," Demetrius admitted with a shudder.

"I don't mind being the boogeyman," Aislinn admitted.

"Yep, you definitely scare me. I think everyone's been wrong all along. You're the evil mastermind. Alex just helps you pull it off and takes credit so everyone looks to you for backup not realizing you're the one they need to watch." Demetrius suggested.

"When we work together the results are more....memorable." Aislinn paused before deciding that asking couldn't hurt. "Did you know it's possible to take things out of the Shadow Realms?" She asked, causing Demetrius to stare at her, mouth agape.

"What? Why?" Demetrius asked.

"I found a journal with a note saying it was from Merrick while in the Shadow Realms. When I woke up it was in my hand." Aislinn explained.

"As far as I know there aren't many cases of that happening but it should be possible. Since Merrick is a Traveler from a different section of the Shadow Realms they should be able to Travel here and leave things in person if they'd like. The reason you can't usually take things back with you when you Travel is that you do so using your astral form and without a physical form you can't carry things." Demetrius said pausing for a moment. "You know what? It's too early for this. I promise to patch things up with Ree and as for your other questions I'll discuss them with you later." Demetrius promised running off before Aislinn could respond.

26.
Alex

Alex arrived to see Aislinn sobbing hysterically struggling to breathe. Alex watched Aislinn in fear before screaming bloody murder. He wished he could help her but didn't know how.

The two of them suffered together while they waited for help to arrive. Eventually, someone came running. He didn't know who it was, but he heard their shoes striking the wood flooring as they rushed toward him. He didn't know when he'd started crying, but he must have because his cheeks were wet and his vision blurry.

Alex felt someone trying to pick him up but he refused to let them. "You have to help her," Alex begged.

"It's okay son. Your mother's got her. It's going to be okay. We're here now." His dad said and he crumpled to the floor as he sobbed.

Alex felt his father lift him and carry him to a chair where he could see Aislinn. Knowing his sister was safe helped but the fear he'd felt at seeing her like that broke something in him.

He never wanted to see her like this again but he didn't know what caused it, or how to fix it. At that moment he vowed to do whatever he could to prevent her from suffering like this again. He hated seeing her so broken. Whatever put that look on her face and made her gasp and cry had to stop. Aislinn was supposed to smile and laugh, not cry, and gasp for air.

After what felt like an eternity he heard Aislinn's sobs die down and her breathing return to normal. The past few days had been terrifying for him. He'd done his best to put on a brave face for Aislinn but he couldn't pretend any longer. Seeing Aislinn continue to break down was the hardest thing he'd ever had to endure. It had broken him and he wasn't sure he could be put back together. With that last depressing thought, Alex cried himself to sleep in his father's arms.

27.
Aislinn

Aislinn woke up in her room at her grandparents' house. She must've been carried here while she slept. She looked around in confusion. Why had she been carried to her room? Her eyes widened in shock as she remembered her breakdown. She wanted to cry but felt too drained to do so.

Aislinn sat up looking down to see if she'd been changed into her pajamas. She hadn't but someone had removed her shoes before tucking her in. She grabbed her shoes, put them on, and headed outside to see if she could find someone willing to answer her questions. She went to the living room. When she got there she saw her parents and grandparents talking.

Before she could say anything her mom rushed toward her pulling her into a tight hug, and carrying her to the couch. Aislinn normally would've felt embarrassed but after what happened she was grateful for the comfort. Her mom picked her up without her having to ask.

"I'm so glad you're alright. You scared me earlier." Her mom admitted, holding back tears.

"I'm sorry," Aislinn said, hiding her face in her mom's sweater.

"I'm just glad I could help. I was so worried about you and all I could do was hold you." Her mom said, hugging her tighter.

"You were the one holding me?" Aislinn asked.

Her mom gasped. "Yes. Who did you think it was?" She asked, sounding odd.

"I didn't know. I couldn't see through the tears and my heart felt like it was going to explode. It was scary. Once it was over I was so tired I didn't care. I remember hearing someone cry." Aislinn admitted.

Her mom let a few tears slip before composing herself. "I'm sorry you were scared. I'd have done anything to spare you that."

"Who was crying?" Aislinn asked.

Her mom looked startled. "You just focus on getting better." Her mom said, trying to keep from answering.

"Who was crying?" Aislinn refused to let it go.

Her mom looked at her with tears in her eyes and shook her head. "She'll find out eventually. It might as well come from us." Her grandmother insisted.

Her mom started to sob in earnest and Aislinn's grandmother picked her up as her father went to comfort her mother. "Will you tell me?" Aislinn asked.

"Alex was crying. We found him screaming while he watched you fall to pieces. Once your mother had you in her arms, your father grabbed him and tried to soothe him. From there; it was a matter of helping the two of you while trying to keep the rest of the kids from seeing you. We still don't know what caused the incident earlier today." Her grandma admitted.

"Is Alex okay?" Aislinn asked.

"We don't know. We finally calmed him down and sent him to bed after you cried yourself out. Rosemary and Paisley have been taking turns checking on you. Now, would you like something to eat? You went to bed before lunch and it's five o'clock. You must be ravenous by now." Her grandma teased.

"I could eat," Aislinn replied.

"Do you have any requests or shall I surprise you?" Her grandma asked.

Aislinn knew she probably wouldn't taste the food anyway, she was too worried about Alex. "Anything's fine," Aislinn replied, sounding sad and tired.

"I'll make you grilled cheese and tomato soup. It'll be nice and soothing. I may even be able to find out where the cookies have been hiding." Her grandma teased.

Aislinn did her best to smile but she could tell it wasn't convincing. "Thanks. Maybe I'll be hungrier when the food's in front of me." Aislinn suggested not wanting her grandma to feel bad about her lack of appetite.

"Why don't you walk beside me. I'll hold your hand so I don't have to worry about losing my balance. You can keep me steady. I'll never need a cane as long as I have grandchildren." Her grandma teased coaxing a real smile out of her.

"Silly grandma. You don't need a cane and you've never had any problems with balancing." Aislinn said before hopping off her grandma's lap and holding out her hand anyway. "But if you insist I promise to help keep you steady," Aislinn promised.

Her grandmother laughed. "You little scamp. What am I going to do with you?" She asked.

"Keep me and love me," Aislinn suggested, prompting both her grandparents to laugh.

"Well, now. That sounds like a fine idea. We certainly shall." Her grandparents declared. "You'll have to break it to your parents though. They seemed certain they'd be taking you home at the end of the summer." Her grandpa teased.

"That's what they want you to think. We're start homeschooling in the fall." Aislinn retorted.

"Where did you learn to maneuver like that?" Her grandma asked, giving her a suspicious glance.

"Mama says I'm pre-co-cious. Alex said it means I'm too smart for my own good." Aislinn replied.

"Well, that's certainly one way to look at it. Let's go make some food. Maybe it'll lure Alex out." Her grandma said leading her to the kitchen.

"Sounds like a plan but do I have to share my cookies?" Aislinn asked, giving her grandma a sly glance.

"You really are a scamp. You'll eat what I serve you and I didn't promise cookies so mind your manners." Her grandma cautioned wagging a finger at her.

"Okay, grandma," Aislinn replied.

"Good." Her grandma declared opening the door to the kitchen. Her grandma flipped on the lights and walked to the cupboards pulling out pots and pans. "Hand me the butter and cheese from the fridge. There should be some soup in the cupboards and fetch me a loaf of bread when you're done." Her grandma suggested.

Aislinn did as she was told, walked over to the table, and sat down. It was one thing to spill milk everywhere but she didn't want to spill soup on herself. "I put everything on the counter for you. Do you need anything else?" Aislinn asked.

"Just keep me company. We can talk while the food is cooking." Her grandma said while prepping a couple of grilled cheese sandwiches and dumping the soup in a pot.

"Okay," Aislinn said, feeling a bit nervous. "Can we talk after the food's done? I don't want to worry about things catching fire because I distracted you." Aislinn explained.

"Okay." Her grandma promised, placing a second sandwich in the pan, and stirring the soup. Her grandma flipped the sandwiches one after the other. When they were done her grandma flipped the sandwiches onto separate plates and spooned some of the soup into a small bowl before taking the plates to the table. She set down the plates and returned to the table with the bowl and a spoon. "It's hot." Her grandma warned.

Aislinn dallied over her sandwich. She was eating as slow as she could but she could barely taste her food. "Eat up. The soup's better warm." Her grandma chided her

"Your food's good, hot or cold." Aislinn insisted before finishing her soup. "I'm done," Aislinn said, taking her dishes to the sink and rinsing them off before putting them in the dishwasher.

"Thank you, dear." Her grandma said before finishing her sandwich and cleaning her dish.

"It's time to talk isn't it?" Aislinn asked, dragging her feet on the way back to the table.

"Sort of. We do need to talk but it doesn't have to be painful." Her grandma motioned for Aislinn to take a seat next to her.

"I'm not so sure," Aislinn muttered, sitting down.

"I'm not going to ask what upset you today. Whatever it was frightened you and while I'd like to know what caused your reaction I don't think now's a good time to ask. So we're going to have a different talk tonight. Has anything like this happened before?" Her grandma asked in a gentle but insistent manner.

"No," Aislinn replied, voice steady.

210

"Good. Will you tell someone if it happens again?" Her grandma asked. Aislinn nodded. "Is there anything bothering you that you're willing to talk about right now?"

Aislinn paused for a few moments. "Rosemary needs help. Thackery's been having problems but we're working on them. You might want to keep an eye on Demetrius. He tried to disappear a few years ago." Aislinn added, making her gasp in shock.

"He tried to run away?" Her grandma asked.

"No. He tried to fall asleep and never wake up." Aislinn admitted.

"Have you told anyone else about this?" Her grandma asked once she'd regained her composure.

"No. With everything going on I'd nearly forgotten about it." Aislinn explained.

"I see. Do you think Demetrius might try again?" Her grandma asked, sounding frightened.

"No. He can't attempt it that way anymore. Haley told some people and they made sure of it. Supposedly it was years ago and isn't a problem anymore but I'm not sure. I don't know why Dee tried it in the first place so I don't know if the problem went away or if he's just being watched too closely to try again." Aislinn admitted.

"I see. I knew about Thackery and Rosemary but I wasn't aware Demetrius needed to be watched. Thanks for letting me know. I'll do my best to ensure he doesn't do anything...foolish." Her grandma promised.

"Thanks," Aislinn said.

The look on her grandma's face was unreadable. "I'm glad I could help." Her grandma said after a long pause.

"No problem." Aislinn went back to looking down at her hands. She'd gone through every distracting topic she could think of and nothing had worked.

"You can't hide forever. Eventually, the truth will out." Her grandma said, shocking her. Was she reading her mind? How had she known?

"You'll think it's stupid," Aislinn muttered staring at the table.

"If it's important to you it's important to me." Her grandma promised. Aislinn wanted to scream. She didn't understand. None of them did.

"I was thinking about Theopolis. The people there seemed so real. I can still hear their screams for help. It felt so real. I just wanted them to be alright. I couldn't help them." Aislinn sobbed.

"Sweetheart, it was just a dream." Her grandma tried to soothe her.

"But what if it wasn't?" Aislinn asked with tear-filled eyes.

"What else could it have been?" Her grandma asked.

Aislinn shook her head crumpling in on herself. "I knew you wouldn't understand." She sobbed running back to her room.

28.
Merrick

Merrick was pleased when they saw Aislinn bouncing atop the green coils which served as grass. Their erstwhile apprentice appeared much more content than the last time they'd spoken.

"Hey. Did you get the journal I left for you?" Merrick asked, raising a fluffy green eyebrow.

"I did. I haven't had a chance to add anything to it." Aislinn admitted.

"It's alright. I bound it to your essence. It'll appear anytime you need it." Merrick said with a smile showing far too many teeth.

"What do you mean you bound the journal to my essence?" Aislinn asked.

"It was the only way to make sure it didn't get left behind when you Traveled. Being your mentor gives me a bit of leeway when it comes to anything related to Traveling. Besides, I needed a way to communicate with you when you left the Shadow Realms." Merrick explained.

"Perhaps in the future, it might be better to let me know when you're messing with my 'essence'," Aislinn said, putting air quotes around the word essence.

"I didn't think it was a big deal," Merrick complained.

"Because you didn't think. Alex trusts you and I trust Alex but that doesn't mean you altering my essence without telling me is okay." Aislinn yelled.

"Are you saying that if I'd told you I was going to bind something to your essence you'd have been fine with it?" Merrick asked in disbelief.

"Probably not, but it would've been better than finding out after the fact. If you'd told me you were going to give me a way to communicate with you and explained how, I would've understood. I don't want you to bind anything to my essence unless it's a matter of life and death. For anything else you need to talk to me." Aislinn insisted glaring at Merrick.

"Why should I?" Merrick asked.

"Because if you don't I'll never trust you again," Aislinn retorted.

"I don't suppose apologizing would help?" Merrick asked.

"It wouldn't hurt but saying you might want to apologize isn't the same as apologizing," Aislinn replied.

"True. I'm sorry I bound the journal to your essence without asking." Merrick said.

"That wasn't too hard was it?" Aislinn asked.

"No, it wasn't. If you've got time we have much to discuss before you return home." Merrick suggested, smiling at the indignant youngling.

"Okay," Aislinn said.

"I've uncovered a few clues for you to add to your journal. The rogue Observers have been rerouting questions about Theopolis since before The Incident." Merrick paused unsure how to word things without frightening the youngling.

"They knew about Theopolis before people started to evacuate?" Aislinn asked.

"Yes. We're hoping we can figure out who benefited from keeping the situation under wraps." Merrick admitted.

"But the Observers are supposed to observe. Doesn't hiding information violate their prime directive?" Aislinn asked.

"It does, but that doesn't seem to bother the people who allowed this atrocity to happen. They had something to gain from the destruction of Theopolis and refused to let anyone interfere. They don't think a youngling is capable of stopping them." Merrick said.

"Just 'cause I'm young doesn't mean they're safe. They shouldn't count on me to keep their secrets." Aislinn declared.

"Good. I don't think you're the Chosen One but I believe you'll play an integral part in the saving of Theopolis." Merrick said.

"Do you think I'll be able to make a difference?" Aislinn asked, staring up at Merrick.

"You already have. If you hadn't found that orb and asked what happened to Theopolis, Alex wouldn't have found out. Alex asked me for help so I got involved and the three of us uncovered the rogue Observers' conspiracy. The Council got involved and now dozens of people know about Theopolis. Eventually, someone will be told who decides to do something and if enough people help, the problem will get fixed. Ultimately it doesn't matter who fixes it, only that it gets fixed." Merrick assured their apprentice.

"Oh. I didn't think what I was doing mattered much." Aislinn admitted.

"Sometimes the smallest actions have the biggest consequences. Life is a lot like throwing a pebble into a pond. It's the ripples which have the biggest effect. So things that seem little now can have big consequences later. Good things multiply as easily as bad things but when kindness reaps dividends the result is nicer than when cruelty reaps dividends." Merrick explained.

"You could've just said all actions have consequences instead of lapsing into a monologue." Aislinn retorted.

"But it wouldn't have sounded as cool," Merrick complained.

"When you try to act cooler than you are, the result is always uncool." Aislinn retorted.

"Alex never says I'm uncool," Merrick said.

"Just because my sibling tolerates your penchant for melodrama doesn't mean I have to," Aislinn replied.

"You wound me most grievously," Merrick whined, acting put

upon.

"Cease your whining. It was a nice bit of hyperbole but the similes were unnecessary. Don't get me wrong. It sounded pretty but it could've been said faster without as much effort. I thought you wanted expedience, especially with so much at stake." Aislinn explained.

"Did you really tell me I added too many words in the wordiest way you could?" Merrick asked sounding incredulous.

"Yes," Aislinn replied.

"Okay, as long as we're clear. Now, do you mind listening while I explain the other things I've uncovered since the last time we talked?" Merrick asked, giving Aislinn a strange look.

"Sure," Aislinn said.

Merrick grinned back. "The conspiracy goes back ages. Part of the reason it's been so hard to track down the original people involved is that there are two kinds of space travel. There's the normal kind which is slow and requires a ton of prep-work and then there's Traveling which is faster and easier. Theon Travelers weren't able to escape Theopolis by Traveling unless they had a method that involved taking their physical body with them." Merrick admitted.

"So the odds of someone escaping by Traveling through the Shadow Realms is slim to none. Anything else?" Aislinn asked.

"It's going to take time to unravel the conspiracy. We don't know whether or not destroying Theopolis was a side effect or the intended result. We don't know if Theopolis' destruction was the final thing the rogue Observers achieved before trying to pin the Chosen One title on you." Merrick added.

"I think I might have a couple of clues to give you," Aislinn admitted.

"Oh. Well, let's hear it." Merrick suggested.

"I ran into a red being when I was about four. An organization was using a planet for experiments. One of the people working there threatened me because I exposed part of their operation. They were turned over to the Council for acts against a youngling and breaking the Traveler's Code. It should be in my file. It may not be related but it might explain why the rogue Observers tried to pin the Savior role on me. They may have thought my natural curiosity would make it hard for me to walk away." Aislinn admitted.

"I hadn't thought about that. How do you expect me to gain access to the files?" Merrick asked.

"You're either an Observer or have infiltrated their ranks. Either way, getting access to a file shouldn't be too hard. If you don't want to tip off the Observers check out the record the Council has. You just gained two apprentices. You should be able to pull our files without raising a fuss. Just claim you want to know what we've accomplished so you know what to teach us." Aislinn suggested.

"You think they'll buy that?" Merrick asked.

"I think you could tell them you wanted to spend time reviewing your apprentice's case files and they'd not only give you a copy of our files but also mention things that didn't make it into the file. If you phrased it properly they might even throw in stuff about our cousins." Aislinn suggested.

"You think adults are that gullible?" Merrick asked.

"No. I just don't think the files of two children are usually classified. They won't protect the information because they don't think it's valuable. As far as the Council knows you're just worried about being a good mentor." Aislinn replied.

"What about this latest situation? Won't they worry about it after that?" Merrick asked.

"It's been like five minutes. They haven't had time to classify anything. As long as you ask before the trial it'll be fine. They'll let you have what's in there because if it's classified then it won't be in the public file." Aislinn explained.

"This isn't exactly what I expected you to say when you told me you had something for me to add to my journal," Merrick admitted.

"Are you shocked I have worthwhile information, that I've stumbled across conspiracies before, or that I gave you an excuse to get into the Council's Hall of Records?" Aislinn asked with a smirk.

"Yes," Merrick answered.

"Drats. I was hoping you'd let me know which one shocked you." Aislinn retorted.

"I wasn't expecting any of the three if I'm being honest. The most surprising part is that you believed me breaking into the Observers'

Hall of Records would be a breeze. You do realize the place is usually locked up tighter than the airlock in a space-faring vessel" Merrick replied.

"Alex snuck in with no problem and he's only eleven." Aislinn retorted.

"You kids are going to give me a complex. I'm not supposed to realize you're better at covert missions than I am until after you've hit puberty." Merrick complained.

"It's not our fault we're naturals at sniffing out corruption, conspiracy, and covert information," Aislinn replied with a wicked grin.

"I suppose I should be lucky I only have to train two of you instead of dealing with your whole family," Merrick admitted.

"You say that like you don't want to deal with all of us. We're much more competent when we're all working together." Aislinn said, trying to make it seem innocuous.

"Somehow that doesn't make me feel any better. If you were trying to reassure me you've failed. It still sounds like a threat. If this is your attempt at seeming cute and innocent I'm surprised you're allowed to do anything unsupervised." Merrick admitted.

"Okay, so I'm not supposed to do most things without being watched but that's true of most children. It doesn't mean all the adults I've met view me as a liability." Aislinn insisted.

Merrick laughed. "Aww. That's cute. You actually believe that."

"That's rich coming from the being who couldn't figure out how to gain access to a place they've either worked for or been infiltrating for years." Aislinn retorted.

"It's official. Your sibling was the easy one. You're the difficult child who makes other adults wonder why your parents didn't stop at one child." Merrick muttered.

"Do you want to say that again a little louder?" Aislinn asked voice soft and menacing.

"I shouldn't have agreed to be a mentor. I've been doing this for less than a week and I'm already arguing with my newest apprentice. Why did I think this was a good idea again?" Merrick asked the universe.

"Because you thought it was the best option at the time and you couldn't think of anything else during a crisis," Aislinn suggested.

"I'd forgotten what it was like to argue with a youngling. Children have the unfortunate tendency to say exactly what they're thinking without any thought for the feelings of others." Merrick remarked still talking more to themself than anyone else.

"No problem. I do think about how my words and actions make other people feel. I just don't always remember to do so before doing something." Aislinn admitted.

"I will try not to play favorites but Alex is easier to get along with," Merrick admitted.

"Do you regret agreeing to teach me?" Aislinn asked.

"I don't regret agreeing to teach you. I just wish I'd thought about it a bit more before saying yes. I wasn't prepared to teach anyone and I hadn't thought about what it would mean to be your mentor. I thought it would be the same as teaching Alex since you two are siblings." Merrick admitted.

"It probably doesn't help that I Traveled here after a breakdown earlier today so I'm more emotional than normal and I still haven't dealt with the reasons for it," Aislinn admitted.

"Do you want to talk about it?" Merrick asked. "You don't have to but it might help."

"You'll think it's stupid," Aislinn said staring at the ground.

"Maybe but you won't know unless you tell me," Merrick said motioning for Aislinn to sit next to them.

Aislinn sat down next to Merrick. "You know I've been Traveling to the Shadow Realms for years right?" Aislinn asked. Merrick nodded. "Well, when I first started Traveling I didn't know what I was doing. I just did it. So when I saw what happened to Theopolis and the Theons I was horrified but it didn't seem fair to be so upset about something I made up. When you gave me the journal it hit me. I took it out of the Shadow Realms which means the Shadow Realms are real and what happens there has real consequences. I freaked out because I found out Theopolis was real." Aislinn explained.

"Most people who end up Traveling were taught to do so at some point. How did you figure it out?" Merrick asked.

"I don't know. I just remember dreaming about going somewhere fun. The first few months of Traveling took me to simple places where I colored or played dress-up. I didn't notice that the people I was meeting looked different. I thought purple was a normal color for humans just like some people on Earth are darker-skinned than others. I'd seen people with fewer limbs than normal so I wasn't shocked when I saw people with an extra limb. Since nobody around me thought it was weird I didn't either." Aislinn admitted.

"Didn't you notice at some point that you were having interactions with aliens?" Merrick asked.

"Yes but by then, I'd seen movies and tv shows about aliens so I thought it was just my imagination showing me images of what I thought aliens should look like," Aislinn replied.

"I see," Merrick said, pausing for a moment. "The shock of learning it was real forced you to acknowledge what the Theons went through. Watching it the way you did was horrifying but you'd done your best to detach yourself from it. When you realized the Shadow Realms were real it was like being traumatized again. You empathized with them and it made the tragedy worse." Merrick mused.

"All I could think about were the screams. I could see the blue fog clinging to everything. I've never felt so horrified in my life. I froze. I couldn't help them and I couldn't look away. All I could do was stand there crying as I witnessed what happened." Aislinn said bursting into tears.

"I'm sorry. I wish you hadn't gone through this. I would've had to explain that the Shadow Realms were real eventually but I'd hoped to do so in a kinder way. Usually, the Travelers who don't know the Shadow Realms are real quit coming to them before it becomes a problem. Most long-term travelers figure it out eventually." Merrick admitted.

"I think I suspected the Shadow Realms were too complex to be imaginary but every time I started to put it together something happened that convinced me I was wrong," Aislinn admitted.

"You're a good kid. You know that right?" Merrick asked.

"I should've done more to help them," Aislinn muttered.

"You're a youngling. It's not your job to save them. It happened long before you were born. There was nothing you could do to prevent it." Merrick assured her.

"Then why do I feel guilty?" Aislinn asked.

"Because you're a good person. You want to help them and you didn't want this to happen to anyone. If it helps, you can keep trying to piece together clues so we can find the people responsible and hold them accountable." Merrick suggested.

"It's not enough to take them to task. Things won't be fixed until Theopolis is inhabitable once more. I want the Theons to return to their home planet." Aislinn declared looking up at Merrick.

"I agree and so does Alex. Between the three of us, we'll be able to find out a lot and we might even be able to convince someone to help us. The more people we get working towards making this happen the easier it will be to accomplish." Merrick explained.

"Do you really think we have a chance at pulling this off?" Aislinn asked.

"Yes. Even if you end up leaving the Shadow Realms behind in a few years I won't. I'll keep working on it and if I retire before fixing this I'll make sure my replacement is notified about this. Whoever is chosen to replace me will be given a list of all my active case files. They'll receive all of my notes and any information I acquired so they'll know anything you pass on to me as well." Merrick said, trying to reassure Aislinn.

"Are you a cop?" Aislinn asked.

"Sort of. I'm kind of like a cross between an Observer and a detective. It's my job to Travel throughout the Shadow Realms trying to make sure nothing really bad happens. Usually, I just watch and compile information but occasionally I step in and try to solve things myself." Merrick explained.

"How often do you step in?" Aislinn asked.

"If I'm lucky a couple of times a year. If not then it's more frequent." Merrick admitted.

"Why would you step in less often if you're lucky? Don't you enjoy being a detective?" Aislinn asked, giving Merrick a weird look.

"If I have to step in and try to solve things directly it's because things have devolved significantly and I'm the only one capable of fixing it. As a Traveler, I'm expected to stay out of things whenever possible. Calling me in early is considered overkill." Merrick admitted.

"Oh. So you're one of the best and giving a case file to you is admitting ordinary detectives can't solve the case." Aislinn said with a smile.

"Pretty much. I also often get cases that are considered unsolvable." Merrick said.

"Why would they give you cases they thought couldn't be solved?" Aislinn asked.

"I can sometimes come up with a solution to a case no-one can crack. Giving me cases I can't solve helps keep my ego in check." Merrick admitted.

"Oh." Aislinn paused for a moment before narrowing her eyes in suspicion. "Did you say this just so you could make a point about how nobody is capable of solving everything?" She questioned.

"Yes," Merrick said without a trace of guilt. "You're still a child and while it's commendable that you want to help, sometimes things can't be solved. I don't want you to wind up broken-hearted because you assumed you were the only one capable of fixing things. You're seven. It's okay for you to fail." Merrick explained.

"You said you thought the situation with Theopolis would be solved." Aislinn accused.

"I do, but I don't think you have to be the one to solve it. The

226

situation with Theopolis is complicated. It's part of a conspiracy that's been going on for eons. We still don't know what happened to Theopolis to cause the blue fog or how to stop it. We don't even know if the planet will be habitable once we remove the blue fog. The Theons haven't lived there in ages and they may have experienced evolutionary changes that make it impossible for them to return to Theopolis." Merrick said quiet but firm.

"It almost sounds like you don't want them to return to their homeworld." Aislinn accused.

"I'd love to be able to tell the Theons they can return home but I'm trying to be realistic here. It's been a long time and we don't know how hard it will be to fix it. I'll settle for uncovering the conspirators who allowed Theopolis to be destroyed. If we can make the blue fog go away and let people inhabit Theopolis again even better. But ensuring the Theons return to their homeworld is more complicated than that. You don't know that they'll want to return. Many of them won't remember Theopolis. They were born off-world and some of them don't even have living relatives who remember Theopolis. It's a place they may not recognize and for many of them it won't matter." Merrick explained.

"How is it that you can agree to mentor an alien child, frequently Traveling between the Shadow Realms but somehow returning the Theons to their homeworld is too unrealistic for you?" Aislinn asked, throwing her hands up in the air.

"I understand how amazing things in the Shadow Realms can be but I don't want you to get hurt if it turns out your dream is impossible. I'd be more than happy to be proven wrong. I'd love to be able to undo the harm that was done to the Theons but I'm not sure it's possible." Merrick admitted.

"What happened to you promising to try?" Aislinn asked.

"I never said I was giving up. I said things aren't always fixable. Honestly, even if the blue fog is removed and the atmosphere of Theopolis is breathable for the Theons, some won't return. Some will have made their home elsewhere. Others will be unable to face the memories Theopolis brings back. Some will feel disconnected, unable to think of Theopolis as home. Finally, there will be the ones who remember Theopolis or the stories their ancestors told about it. Some will feel it is the home they've been searching for but never found. You can't expect all of the Theons to feel the same way about something. There are too many people and cultures for that to be possible. Very few things result in a unified response." Merrick explained.

"Is it bad that I wanted them to return?" Aislinn asked.

"No. But the Theons get to make their own choices. What happened to Theopolis was terrible but not everyone who can trace their ancestry back to Theopolis will want to live on Theopolis. You can't make up their minds for them." Merrick insisted.

"Does that mean I shouldn't try to make Theopolis livable again?"

Aislinn asked.

"No. Theopolis used to be a thriving planet with a rich culture and interplanetary renown. Their marketplaces were incredible and beings used to travel just for a chance to glimpse Theopolis. It doesn't help that you've been calling the natives of Theopolis Theons. It makes them sound more unified than they were. Theon used to mean a native of the planet Theopolis. They had their own names for the different species who called the place home. It's been so long only the descendants are likely to remember the individual names for the species and cultures that are now called Theons." Merrick explained.

"Sort of like how I'm a Traveler or Terran Traveler from the planet Earth, even though I think of myself as from a particular subsection of Earth," Aislinn said.

"Yes. You wouldn't expect everyone on Earth to have the same feelings you do." Merrick said, feeling proud of their apprentice.

"No. I wouldn't." Aislinn said looking down at the grass.

"I don't expect you to be perfect. You just have to remember to keep an open mind." Merrick chided.

"I will." Aislinn paused a moment. "I won't always get it right the first time but I can promise to try not to repeat my mistakes."

"Just do your best and try to improve," Merrick suggested.

"If some of the Theons don't want to go back to Theopolis will the planet be open to non-Theons?" Aislinn asked.

"I'm not sure. It depends on what people decide to do about

Theopolis once it's fixed. If the atmosphere is breathable again a committee will be formed to decide what to do about it. I'm fine with any of the possibilities as long as the Theons agree and everyone seems happy." Merrick admitted.

"I hope Theopolis becomes a home again. I don't want it to be taken over by soulless corporations. It would feel wrong to have people profiting from tragedy." Aislinn declared.

"I'm sure the committee will take it into consideration but ultimately unless one of us winds up on the committee we won't have much of a say in what happens," Merrick admitted.

"Still seems rude to try and profit off of the destruction of a planet." Aislinn insisted.

Merrick nodded but before they could say anything Aislinn's eyes widened. "I should head home. I've been here too long and I will need some actual sleep before waking up." Aislinn admitted.

"Fair enough. Sleep well and remember neither you nor Alex are expected to solve things on your own." Merrick said before Aislinn vanished.

29.
Aislinn

Aislinn woke up thinking of Merrick's words. 'Neither you nor Alex are expected to solve things on your own.' What did they mean? Who was expecting Alex to solve things on his own? She shook her head trying to clear her mind. Maybe it would help if she asked Alex. She wanted to talk to him about the journals anyway.

Aislinn got out of bed and dressed in jeans and a striped shirt. Her hair was a mess but she'd worry about it later.

She walked towards the kitchen and saw Alex. "We've got a lot to talk about. Have you seen any of the adults?" Aislinn asked.

"No. I made myself some cereal." Alex admitted.

"Merrick told me the journals they gave us are anchored to our essence and can't be lost. You should've found yours but if you haven't; thinking about it should summon it." Aislinn explained.

"Did Merrick tell you anything else?" Alex asked.

"Merrick learned this isn't the first conspiracy I've uncovered. They're going to ask the Council for our files. Merrick wants to compare the information in the Council files with what's in the

Observers' files." Aislinn said.

"Makes sense," Alex admitted.

"Any idea why Merrick said neither of us are expected to solve things on our own?" Aislinn asked.

"We do tend to band together and forget to ask for help. If it makes you feel better we can add it to the list of clues we're collecting." Alex suggested.

"Merrick told me not to get upset if I don't manage to make Theopolis inhabitable again. I forgot that just because the Theons had ancestors who lived on Theopolis doesn't mean they will want to return." Aislinn admitted looking at the ground.

"It's okay. I hadn't thought about that either." Alex admitted.

"Really? You're not just trying to make me feel better?" Aislinn asked giving him a suspicious look.

"Honest. I hadn't thought about whether or not the Theons would return. I was just horrified by what happened to Theopolis. When I think about the screams I can almost hear them." Alex shuddered. "I don't think I've ever been so afraid in my life. Watching that blue fog creeping in was horrible. I've never seen anything so insidious. I don't think I'll ever be able to look at anything blue and syrupy again without feeling frightened." Alex admitted.

"Why didn't you tell me it scared you?" Aislinn asked.

"I didn't want to make you feel worse," Alex admitted.

"Why would I feel worse?" Aislinn asked.

"The only reason I found out about Theopolis is that you were upset by it. I just wanted to help you," Alex admitted.

"Knowing I'm not alone helped. I thought I was being a baby since I couldn't handle it." Aislinn admitted.

"What happened was terrible. You're allowed to feel however you need to about what happened. I'm four years older and the only reason I haven't spent every day since crying is because I've been trying to help you." Alex admitted.

"So I'm not a baby," Aislinn said feeling as if a weight had been lifted off her chest.

"Of course not." Alex declared pulling her into a hug. "Your heart is hurting because other people were hurt. I have never been so proud to be your brother." Alex declared smiling at her.

"Because I cried?" Aislinn asked.

"Because after everything that's happened since you discovered the fate of Theopolis you still want to help the Theons. You're not whining about what happened to you. You just decided you were going to help." Alex explained.

"Huh, I guess I did," Aislinn said sounding shocked.

"It's why I'm proud of you. It would've been easier to curl up in a ball crying and feeling sorry for yourself." Alex continued.

"I've been crying and cowering off and on since I found out," Aislinn admitted.

"Doesn't stop me from being proud of you. Being upset and scared doesn't make you less of a good person. Everyone cries sometimes. Besides even if I wanted to make fun of you for being traumatized, which I don't, I'd wind up insulting myself at the same time. When this happened I wasn't worried about the Theons or Theopolis. I just wanted you to be alright. You're the one who managed to look past your own pain and realize they needed help." Alex admitted.

"You do realize you're eleven right?" Aislinn asked giving her brother a strange look.

"What does that have to do with anything?" Alex asked.

"Eleven-year-olds aren't expected to be compassionate. Once you had time to process and see the bigger picture you decided to help just like I did." Aislinn explained glaring at Alex.

"When did you get so smart?" Alex asked.

"When I started Traveling and learned there was more to the universe than I thought.." Aislinn explained.

"You know, there's a reason you're my best friend, but don't tell mom and dad," Alex said.

"True. They won't bribe us to get along if they know they don't need to." Aislinn admitted.

"Seriously, though. Thanks for kicking me out of my funk." Alex said with a smile.

"No problem," Aislinn said.

"Are you okay?" Alex asked.

"No, but I will be. I just want a few hours without a crisis so I can relax." Aislinn said, giving her brother a wan smile.

"I'm gonna head to the Shadow Realms for a bit. If you need me before I get back you can use your journal to send me a message." Alex suggested.

30.
Alex

Alex waited for his sister to leave and then traveled trying to focus on finding a peaceful realm. He found himself on a polka dot planet. Everything was covered in polka dots of varying shades. He didn't know how long he'd been resting when he saw a Traveler coming towards him and realized it was his sister.

"How did you get here?" Alex asked.

"I just focused on finding you. The Shadow Realms are a good place to talk without being overheard." Aislinn replied.

"You're attempting to uncover a conspiracy and you have no way of knowing if someone is listening," Alex said.

"I think the rogue Observers are keeping their heads down. They know if they get caught they'll be locked up and their entire organization will get busted. Besides, I'm not here to talk about that." Aislinn paused. "I may have made a mistake. I was talking to grandma and I said something I shouldn't have. Please don't hate me." Aislinn pleaded.

Alex blinked at her for a minute. "I won't hate you. Just tell me what happened. We'll figure it out from there." Alex promised.

"I was trying to avoid explaining why I freaked out and so I started saying anything I could to divert her attention. I told her about Rosemary and Thackery and when she wouldn't let up I told her..." Aislinn paused.

"What?" Alex said.

"I told her what Demetrius tried to do," Aislinn admitted.

"Good." Alex declared.

"I told his biggest secret to grandma to avoid talking to her. How is that good?" Aislinn demanded.

"What Demetrius said scared me. I'm glad you told grandma. It saves me the trouble of doing it." Alex insisted.

"Why aren't you mad at me for narking?" Aislinn asked.

"Because whether Dee wants to admit it or not what he attempted was dangerous. It's not the kind of secret he can ask us to keep. Haley might think it's over but he's been wrong before. If Haley knew Demetrius was upset he wouldn't have let it go so far. Besides, there's more than one way to do what Demetrius attempted. I'll talk to one of the adults before we head home so if Demetrius gets mad he'll blame me." Alex suggested.

"You're not worried he'll hate you?" Aislinn asked.

"It's a price I'm willing to pay. I'd rather him hate me and be safe than love me and get hurt." Alex declared.

"Thanks," Aislinn said, pulling Alex into a hug.

"No problem," Alex promised.

"I'm glad you're my brother," Aislinn said, ending the hug.

"If Demetrius' secret wasn't hurting anyone he'd have a right to be mad but everything you mentioned was causing people pain. Did you tell grandma anything else I should know about?" Alex asked.

"I asked her what I should do if it wasn't a dream. I didn't want to pretend anymore and I figured if she was a Traveler I could tell her everything." Aislinn admitted.

"You know adults can't usually Travel." Alex reminded her.

"I know but I was hoping grandma and grandpa might be different," Aislinn admitted.

"What did she say?" Alex asked.

"She asked what else it could be. She didn't understand so I ran back to my room and Traveled to avoid her." Aislinn admitted.

"What are you going to do if she asks what you meant?" Alex asked.

"Tell her it felt real and I can still hear the Theons screaming. I see Theopolis being destroyed when I close my eyes. I'm afraid to go to sleep because I'll see it again. I wish it was over but it's not." Aislinn said bursting into tears.

Alex sighed and pulled Aislinn into his arms for a hug. "It's okay to be afraid. I know I am. We'll figure something out." Alex promised.

"You're just saying that aren't you?" Aislinn asked.

"If I was I'd have told you Merrick will fix everything or that I'd solve it for you. The more people working to solve this the better the odds are. Eventually, someone will find the rest of the rogue Observers and expose the conspiracy." Alex promised.

"Thanks. I wasn't sure I'd be able to fix this on my own." Aislinn admitted.

"You don't have to." Alex insisted.

"If you focus on your notebook I can show you what I've discovered already and we can see if Merrick's uncovered anything new," Aislinn suggested reaching for her notebook.

Alex furrowed his brows and a few minutes later his notebook was in his hands. "Wow. I wasn't sure that would work." Alex admitted.

"I told you so didn't I?" Aislinn asked.

"You did but hearing about it's different than seeing it." Alex replied before gasping.

"What is it?" Aislinn asked.

"It's time to head back. Mom's calling me for dinner. We'll talk more later." Alex said before Traveling back home, hoping his sister would follow him home.

31.
Aislinn

Aislinn woke up feeling determined to fix things. Her journey wasn't over. It had just begun. She was going to help the Theons any way she could. If that meant learning things so she could pass them on, she would. For now, that would have to be enough.

She'd need to be smarter to reach her goal. Even her mentor thought she'd outgrow her dream. Maybe it wasn't the future she'd wanted, but dreams can change, and so can plans.

If she wanted to make a difference, she could. She had access to the Shadow Realms and the whole multiverse at her fingertips. If she couldn't save a planet with those kinds of resources then nobody could. She didn't have to be the hero. Nobody said heroes had to solve things on their own.

Aislinn smiled. She wasn't sure why things felt so much easier this morning. She still felt the weight of others' expectations, but today the load felt lighter and the sun seemed brighter. She didn't know if she'd met the Chosen One, or even if she would, but knowing she could help them made it okay.

In the confines of her mind, she knew she didn't want to be the Chosen One. The stakes were too high and she didn't know enough to make things right. She just wanted to help and make a difference, even if no one ever knew.

Everything in her life was leading up to this moment. It didn't matter that there was a group of people trying to stop her or how hard it would be. The odds were stacked against her, but the odds had never faced her before.

She wasn't doing this alone. She had Alex and Merrick and all of her cousins. Somewhere in the Shadow Realms, the answers were hiding and she was going to find them. Aislinn smiled. If there was one thing she was good at; it was finding out things. Being a kid involved a lot of being told you were *"too young"* to know something or worry about it. She'd never believed that before, and she wasn't about to start now.

Those conspirators didn't know who they were up against. She was a Smith and her cousin was still Traveling at fifteen. She had at least eight more years of Traveling before she had to worry about quitting. Some beings Traveled well into adulthood. Who's to say she couldn't do the same?

It was amusing how easy it was to start on a lifelong quest. She wasn't sure she'd quit searching for answers and trying to help people even if she did save Theopolis. She knew it could take years but she wasn't going to wait that long to make a difference.

There was plenty of work to do both in the Shadow Realms and on Earth. Her cousins Thackery and Dee needed help, as did Aunt Rosemary. And those were just the problems affecting her family.

She could do this. She would do this. The world didn't know it, but this day would determine the rest of her life. Revolutions can't start without preparation, so Aislinn got out of bed, got dressed, and headed to the kitchen. Life-changing moment or not, she needed food before anything else happened.

www.ingramcontent.com/pod-product-compliance
Lightning Source LLC
Chambersburg PA
CBHW072226190626
46809CB00017B/814